THE WHITE WOMAN

Liam Davison was born in Melbourne in 1957. His first novel, *The Velodrome*, was shortlisted for the 1987 *Australian*/Vogel Award and his collection of stories, *The Shipwreck Party*, was published by UQP in 1989. His short fiction has been widely published and broadcast and has received a number of awards and prizes. His second novel *Soundings* was shortlisted for the Victorian Premier's Award and won the National Book Council Banjo Award for Fiction in 1993. He lives on the Mornington Peninsula with his wife and two children, and teaches fiction writing at the Frankston college of TAFE. During 1993 he travelled in Italy and France after winning the Marten Bequest Travelling Scholarship. *The White Woman* was written with the assistance of the Literature Board of the Australia Council and the Victorian Ministry of the Arts.

Other books by Liam Davison

The Velodrome
The Shipwreck Party
Soundings

THE WHITE WOMAN

LIAM DAVISON

University of Queensland Press

First published 1994 by University of Queensland Press
Box 42, St Lucia, Queensland 4067 Australia

Typeset by University of Queensland Press
Printed in Australia by McPherson's Printing Group

Cataloguing in Publication Data
National Library of Australia

Davison, Liam, 1957–   .
   The white woman.

   I. Title.

A823.3

ISBN 0 7022 2680 7

Unhappiest of the fairer kind;
Who knows the misery of thy mind —
What tongue thy grief can tell?
Torn from kind parents, friends and home,
And left in the wild woods to roam —
With savages to dwell.

Ode To The White Woman
HOMO, *Argus,* 7 September 1847

The natives are very numerous, and no person but those well acquainted with Gipps Land can form the least idea of the nature of the country, which consists of dense scrubs, lakes, rivers, islands, mountains, morasses, and other impediments; and they frequent the most inaccessible parts, in consequence of being so constantly hunted by the native police and settlers should they dare to appear on any forest land.

Christian J. DeVilliers
Commandant, White Woman Expedition
Argus, 26 January 1847

ACKNOWLEDGMENTS

I would like to acknowledge the work of Mr W.J. Cuthill in compiling the extensive collection of manuscript material, *The White Woman Manuscripts*, held by the LaTrobe Library, Melbourne. They were an invaluable resource when researching this novel.

I would like to thank the Literature Board of the Australia Council, the Federal Government's arts funding and advisory body, for its generous support during 1992 and the Victorian Ministry of the Arts for the assistance it provided to research the novel.

Much of this work was completed while in receipt of the Marten Bequest Travelling Scholarship for prose which is gratefully acknowledged.

As always, I would also like to thank my family for their patience and support.

An extract from this novel was first published, in a slightly different form, in *Manoa: A Pacific Journal of International Writing* published by the Department of English at the University of Hawaii.

1

You come here asking about your father. Did I know him? Can I tell what he was like? Do I remember the things we did? The answer's yes, and yes, and yes again. Every time, it's yes, though you might wish you hadn't asked. We travelled together. We shared the same cramped tent at nights, breathed in each other's breath, drew warmth from each other's bodies. Yes, I remember the things he said. But these were fearful times. You have to understand. There were things which couldn't be uttered, dark things that swelled beneath our talk but never broke. You ask about him as though there's nothing I can't reveal. You think it's finished? Consider what might be at stake. You think that all I have to do is speak and the story will unfold. It's not that simple.

Sometimes, when we were out there, we sat for hours beneath the dark sky not uttering a word, or we lay awake listening to each other breathe. And we both knew where we stood. We both knew what had gone before. There was no need to translate it into words and burden each other with the responsibility of having heard it said. Don't think the same won't apply to you. Do you really want it told? Yes, it concerns you. How can it not, being your father's son?

I should be asking what you already know: how well you knew him, how much he told of the years before your birth. I should ask what you've really come here for. You see, there are still things which shouldn't be revealed. But I won't ask. I won't put you to the test. Because it's not your father who's brought you here. It's not him you've come looking for at all, is it? It's her.

I can see it in the way you avert your eyes, the way they flick nervously about my room in search of some tell-tale sign of her even as we speak. You half expect her to materialise before you. I can hear it too, in the way you ask your questions, the way you hedge around your topic like a sheepdog yapping at the heels of it, teasing it. You avoid the questions you most want to ask.

Perhaps it's just as well. It's fear that does it. You remind me of a man poking at a fire with a stick when what you really want to do is thrust your hand into its middle and clasp the coals. Don't worry. I know fear. It's a terrible thing. It won't leave you alone, won't let you rest. It's what she does to you. She keeps niggling at your thoughts until you snap. Others will tell you the same. No doubt you've already asked. I won't flatter myself by thinking mine is the only story you've asked to hear. I should be asking you the questions. You have it all you see, or will have by the time you've finished. All the different perspectives. History you'll call it, all the more truthful for having all the angles; all the more sceptical.

Don't worry, I won't disappoint you. I have a story to tell, though it might not be the one you want to hear. No doubt you'll alter it to suit, or choose what you want to hear — which bits will become history and which will not. I'll tell you my truth anyway for what it's worth; the truth I hold to. Oh yes, I still believe in truth, just as I still believe in her. It's in here you see, inside this wizened head of mine. If you could crack it open you'd see it shining there like silver, though I doubt that anyone could hold it. It would slip through your fingers like the slime it floated in. Your father could tell you about that — about cracking heads and the mess it makes. But that's not what you've come to hear.

I'll tell you about her. I'll tell you, without you having to ask, about the things we did for her, the unspoken and the unspeakable, which is the only way I can tell about your father. That should make it easy for you. Take only what you need. Pretend not to hear if you wish. Leave the room if you'd feel more comfortable. It's only talk. It isn't history yet. You don't have to believe a word I say.

Where would you like me to begin? The start? The end? That's the problem with the past — the choice it offers. The advantages of hindsight. Things don't unfold before your eyes. You have to give it shape. And even then, when you think you've got it nailed — the right events in the clearest possible order — it squirms into the present and changes things. It should be settled but it isn't. Don't I still see her? Still hear her voice? Don't I reach out for her in the middle of the night, just as you must reach out to touch your own wife and find her reassuringly beside you? No, I never married. Commitment, you see. Or fear of it. And don't tell me you don't see her too, in your own wife, your own daughter. Isn't that why you've come?

No, it isn't settled. Not yet. It should have finished when they found her bones shoved inside that hollow tree. "*No room for doubt to dwell in the mind of even the most sceptical,"* the papers said. *"The remains of the captive white woman, butchered on the shores of Lake King at the hands of savages. Death descending as a blessing upon this poor woman, who has undergone a trial far more harrowing and terrible than even death's worst moments."*

See how the papers handled it; how they brought her to life again with words. There's a story for you if it's the one you want. Read the papers. They created us. They gave us life.

"White Woman Expedition Departs." "Great Hopes Held for Her Imminent Rescue." "The Happy Band of Bold Adventurers: brave men willing to risk their lives without fee or reward but that of self-approval."

See how they had us setting out in search of her, weighed down not only with our whaleboats and trinkets for the blacks, but with all the hopes and fears of our still-young colony. They made crusaders out of us. Expeditioners they called us. It was more than an expedition. It was a Quest!

They knew how to make the language work. *"Our sacred duty!"* The pictures they painted. The high emotion of it all. How they could make us feel guilty for something we'd never done, or shame or anger or bring the blood boiling in our veins with outrage for what might have happened to her! Oh yes, the papers tell a story.

Here, I've kept a scrapbook — all the yellowing pages of her harrowing ordeal. *"The horrors of such a captivity. The helpless misery of her wretchedness."* But it's not that simple is it? It all looks so neat in the ordered lines, the two-inch columns. A date for every episode. *"An inquest was duly held on the bodies. There could not be an atom of doubt of one of*

4

them being that of a white female, which was easily evident from her head."

Can you imagine it, the task of identifying the bones? There wasn't much in the way of skin they said, not enough to determine what colour it might once have been. But there was hair. Not flaming red as it was meant to be but enough of it still clinging to the scalp to aid the doctor in telling whose it was. Can you imagine him sorting through the bones? Can you see him drawing them one by one from the tree in the blazing heat and laying them out in front of him, reconstructing the shape of her on the ground? And the flies swarming and the stench of it gagging in his throat? A grisly business it would have been. More detective work than doctoring, not unlike what you're doing now. Raking through the bones. Bringing it back to life.

See how the jaw fits comfortably to the skull. If it could speak ... see how the knuckles would have held the slender finger bones in place. They're still pliant. Feel them. They bend like green wood. And the vertebrae. There's still beauty there, still grace — each segment fitting perfectly to the next. See how he lays them out. The line of it! And the thin cage of her ribs bowing towards you like the hull of a well-constructed boat. He pulls the broken bones into place. The heart would sit just there. There. Slip your hand in between and make a fist. Yes, like that. That's the size of it. Just there.

Don't think I'm not familiar with the Heart; the shape of it cut into the earth; the enormity of the meaning behind it — a white woman held captive by the blacks. That's where it started isn't it? The shape of a heart, the remains of a brass sextant, a pair of prunella shoes. That's where it all began. Is

5

that where we'll start now? Do you really want to dig it up again? Is it really what you want? I'll make some tea.

Yes, we could start at the beginning. Less messy than the other end — a definite date, agreement on the site, initials cut into a tree. It's the ending we can't get right. That's why you're here. It should have finished with her bones, the headlines in the paper:

"EXTRAORDINARY." Friday, 5 November 1847. *"She is no more. The public suspense has been at length relieved."*

But it hasn't, has it? You're still here. Nothing's been resolved. There was that woman who came screaming from the bush years later, all wide-eyed and shock-haired, never to utter a word in English before she died. And later again, that missionary fellow saw her beckoning to him across the lake. Can you imagine it, the faith he must have had? The vision of her? A white woman standing on the water. Can you believe what the mind throws up?

The rumours still persist. Even now there's men who'll claim to see her. Out there on the edges of the runs; a week out from home perhaps with night closing in and the sounds of unnamed creatures moving through the bush, a stockman or shepherd will see her and something inside of him will stir. He might speak, or keep it to himself, or take his gun, but something will stir as it did for me. Fear perhaps, or longing, or the need to believe. Something will hold him to the task of finding her. Because, you see, there was never agreement on the bones, never any certainty that it was her.

Some said it was a lubra and her child. Can you see the irony of that? The good doctor piecing her together, handling the bones like relics, and all along she was what we were

6

trying to protect her from. As if we hadn't seen enough of their bones to tell one of theirs from ours!

No, it didn't finish there. There's nothing neat or final about it, nothing you can put your finger on without it sliding out from under it. It was like that even then — nothing straightforward, nothing you could get a grip of. Each time we thought we had her within reach, so close we could almost feel the soft touch of her flesh against us, she'd disappear again into the mountains or the dark tracts of inaccessible bush behind the lakes. Picture the size of it. How small she seemed. How huge our task: to journey into that vast expanse of wilderness with only the most rudimentary of maps to guide us, the most unreliable of assistants; to say, "Yes. This is where she will be."

We followed the rivers in, holding to their banks, hoping against hope that they would somehow bring us to her. Not all kept their faith. I'm not sure they all had faith to start with. McLeod, for instance, started to doubt she ever existed at all but went along, wanting to believe, wanting to be proved wrong.

You have to understand what the times were like — the uncertainties we faced, the fear. When we first arrived at Raymond's station there was a cannon pointed into the bush. Behind it was Lake Wellington and the house; before it, nothing but scrub. Isolation. Even in Melbourne with its grid of streets and churches half-finished on the corners, we felt it: the absolute isolation of the place. There was the feeling that we'd somehow cut ourselves adrift from everything that made us what we were.

You could see it in the streets, the effect the place was having on us I mean: the drunkenness, the small perversions, the public squabbling which took the place of conversation. There were too many men together. Things were not as they should have been. Yes, there were libraries, courts of law, a church for every denomination, a School of Arts. But there was the fear that none of it would hold; that the land itself had somehow tarnished us. We'd seen it in the government's response, its abrogation of its duty.

"We remain unconvinced that there is sufficient evidence of her existence to warrant the expenditure of such a sum as would be required to mount an extensive search."

Unconvinced! They spoke to us of conviction. A Christian government prepared to leave her to her fate. Such barbarism, such inhumanity, when even the slightest possibility of a white woman enduring such a plight should have been enough to move them. Civilization! You see how far we'd come? There was the chance that everything would slip away unless we dragged it back and reclaimed ourselves.

You see how much we needed her, how powerless we really were? For all the papers said, for all the preparations we made to rescue her — the public meetings, the inventories of stores and guns and uniforms, the endless words investing us with power — it was she who drew us out there. It was she who left us wandering aimlessly through the scrub, pointing our guns at anything that moved. Once she had us there was nothing we could do, and the closer we got to her, the less certain we became of whether we wanted her at all.

Oh yes, we needed her, but not like that. Not on her terms. It wasn't the blacks we should have feared. It wasn't the land, for all the hostility it showed us. It was her.

We had to go out there, you see. We had to act. And don't you presume to judge, not by your own standards. You have to see it through our eyes and, when all is said and done, you can't. Not because there's so much you don't know, but because there's so much you do. You can't black it out or draw yourself in to see things the way we did. You can't deny your knowledge. All you can do is search for more, and the more you search, the further away from us you get — the further away from her.

But I can see you want to hear. You're impatient for it. Yes, I'll start. I'll start with our first attempt to find her. I wasn't with your father then, but I saw the signs of where he'd been — the broken carbine clotted with hair and skin, the trampled grass, the bodies lying in the bush. Yes, I'll tell you what we did. Drink your tea. Listen.

2

There was a performance when we left, what with the newspapers, and the constables taking Billy Lonsdale into custody the night before. I was below deck with Hartnett and McLeod, stowing our belongings in the cramped quarters of the Shamrock, when they came for him. The blacks were all on deck. McLeod was unhappy about them being on board at all. He'd given them a wide berth before coming below and had spat on the deck to show his contempt. Hartnett was the opposite. He spent more time with them than he did below deck, trying to learn their words and writing them down in a small book he carried with him.

McLeod eyed the book with obvious disgust. An abomination he called it once, as if the words themselves might somehow contaminate the ship. Hartnett wrote their names down too: Yal-Yal and Parram-Bullong — their real names, and the tribes they'd come from. Lonsdale was a Boonoorong. He was sitting there smoking with the other blacks by all accounts when the constables marched along the dock and dragged him away. We heard the scuffle from below and McLeod reached for the carbine he'd carried on board, thinking they'd started to turn already.

Hartnett was first on deck but Lonsdale was already off the boat with a knot of press men following him along the dock. They could have taken him any time they wanted — disturbing the peace or some such black man's charge they had him on. But they waited. Made a spectacle of it, you see. Anything to sully our reputations.

McLeod, of course, was glad to see him go. "Should have taken the whole damn lot," he said. And Hartnett, I suspect, was more upset at the loss of a Boonoorong to observe than at any injustice that might be done. Most of our blacks were Melbourne blacks you see, Wurundjeri. It was something different to see the Boonoorongs at work, especially down in Gippsland. There was no love lost. Not that McLeod saw any difference. "Black is black," he said. "Better off without them."

Yes, it was an ignoble start to our expedition. Not everyone was behind us, you understand. Not like those grand departures of expeditions in search of pasture land or new routes to the north. There were no bands or processions through the streets; no glorious visions of progress. Only shame and guilt. Many would have preferred we let her rest. The government made its contribution the day we left: three oars per order of Captain Lonsdale.

We were easy targets for ridicule: poorly equipped, dependent on subscriptions, inexperienced in the bush. We took two boats and barely a sailor amongst us! Yes, I can see how they laughed. Dingle arrived with his rosary beads rattling at his side. Warman strutted aboard in new boots, saluting to the press.

"We'll do the job," he said.

There were six of us in all with Christian DeVilliers in

charge. He welcomed us aboard with a small, aristocratic bow. That was part of his appeal — his foreignness, the different way he did things. His French accent was still strong. And because his life was defined by a language we didn't understand, it seemed somehow more important than our own. He'd done things we could hardly comprehend. What sort of man resigns twice from the Native Police? You have to wonder what he knew. What enticed him back?

Officially he was sympathetic to the blacks; too soft perhaps for the job. But there were rumours about him too: poisoned flour; blacks hankering for revenge; settlers anxious to see him out of Gippsland. There were plenty who thought him unsuited to lead the expedition. Perhaps it *was* that he knew too much. He stood there with a great watch and chain looped across his breast like a military honour, welcoming us aboard, seemingly in control. But when it came time to leave he didn't act. Warman was all but freeing the ropes himself. The Captain watched the tide slip past its prime. For all the papers said about DeVilliers' commitment to our cause, he seemed unwilling to give the order.

Most action, I think, is the result of seeing one side more clearly than the other. DeVilliers was caught somewhere in between. If he had a responsibility to act, he could also see the consequences, just as he could see the consequences of doing nothing at all. The rest of us had ignorance on our side. We could believe, you see. For DeVilliers it was never anything but duty.

When he eventually spoke and the *Shamrock* slipped away from the wharf, there was a small group of well-wishers huddled on the dock, waving as the Captain steered us into the channel. Most of them were women. We were their only hope, see. They'd put their money in: a pound here, a guinea there, ten pounds raised from a charity tea, and now it was up to us to bring her home. They must have contemplated the horrors she endured and prayed to have her back among them, safe in their parlours where she belonged. What a prize she'd be! To have her sitting there, poor girl, sipping tea. Saved from a dreadful fate by their own generosity.

Even before we'd left, they'd started to make their plans: the guest lists, the subjects to be cautiously avoided. They'd staked their claims, and who could argue that they had a right to her after all the years of isolation they'd endured themselves, removed from the centres of civilisation? No doubt they saw themselves in her. They were entitled to a cause.

And the press were there of course. A smaller group standing to one side with their pens in hand. It was them who had set it up. Exclusive rights for the *Herald*; Cavenagh made sure of that. That's what we were, you see: a story. Each stage of our journey was a new instalment. Letters home from De Villiers. Odds taken on how long we'd take to find her. They couldn't lose, even if we never came close. It was the story they were after.

Look, *"all fired by a common sense of purpose, the expeditioners set sail from Williamstown at first light"*. See how it simplifies things, how it works to lift the story. It's the kind of language Cavenagh liked to use. And the thing is, we believed it. There was no doubt in my mind that we were all setting out with the same unquestionable motive. I was younger than you are now. I still believed in absolutes. Even now, reading over the stories Cavenagh wrote about us for a gullible populace, it's hard not to believe they're true.

The real past slips elusively from memory while what he

wrote holds fast. Cavenagh told them what they wanted to hear. We were characters, you see, waiting for the plot to unfold before us. We watched the land slide past in the distance — the blank wall of bush behind the line of surf, the rivers opening into it — and wondered what signs we'd find to follow.

The coast stretched endlessly before us, shrouded in what looked like mist from the pounding waves. Behind it, the mountains were barely visible. Such a huge expanse of land! I tried to imagine us standing on the beach with the roar of the waves behind us, calling her name into it. And the thing is, we didn't have a name to call.

Some said it was Mrs Capel, wife of a Sydney brewer, ten months enceinte when the *Britannia* went down. Some said Ellen McPherson. Others clung to Miss Lord, eldest daughter of a failed merchant. Can you imagine us calling out for her, shouting that name into the godless bush? It might have been any one of them or any one of a dozen more. *Britannia*, *Britomart*, *Yarra-Yarra*, *Sarah*. All went down along that stretch of coast. All had women aboard.

There were rumours of course, stories which couldn't be discounted. She was the educated daughter of an English lord; the mother of children; a child herself. She had entered religious orders. In the end, all we had was the name the blacks had given her. *Lohantuka*. White woman. To be honest, I fear she was something different to each of us; mother, daughter, lover, wife. Or all of them.

The blacks refused to go below deck. They spent the night above us, looking out across the water at the land. God knows what they thought of us, dragging them out there, providing them with clothes and rations. If truth be told, I would have rathered they weren't there. On that I sided with McLeod. Always the question of allegiances, you see. Always the question of trust. There was the feeling they might have been laughing at us too. But you see the position we were in, how little power we really had? At least we didn't issue them with guns.

Did I tell you, I dreamed of her that first night, with the Southern Ocean rolling beneath the boat and the blacks mumbling above us? I saw her shining above the mast with a red corona of hair about her face. The wind moaned and hummed through the rigging and I heard it as her voice singing us in to land. She led us through a safe passage between the churning waves to a stretch of beach so white we could barely look at it. From there I saw her beckoning us into the bush, and all around her the leaves and branches quivered with light as if they were ready to burst into flame. As she moved away from us I saw black figures rising from the scrub on either side of her.

She was perfect, as I'd always imagined her to be. There was never any doubt in my mind that such perfection could exist. Once, before the stories of her captivity came to light, I advertised for a wife. I placed notices in the public papers. *"Virtuous woman of good moral standing. Nineteen to twenty-five years of age. Well groomed, fair of complexion, softly spoken."* I'd been searching for her all along, you see. *"Red or auburn haired. Maternal. Domestically inclined. Required by Gentleman of independent means."*

I offered security and comfort. I could have protected her. I believed that then. I believed I could have saved her from it all if she'd only come to me. But of course, she didn't. There was no response to my notices at all. Then the stories started to circulate — by word of mouth at first then in the papers, *"White Woman Held Captive by the Gippsland Blacks"*, and everyone was onto her.

I can see now that I expected too much. Most likely she was still in England when I first reached out, still safely cosseted in her parents' garden. What need did she have of my protection? What could I possibly have offered her? The decision to travel to this place with all its uncertainties and fears had not been made. She couldn't have known how much I wanted her. It's only now that I can see how foolish I was, how lovesick with the idea of her. Yes, I call it love. She was mine you see, long before the expedition set out.

Then there was your father. I found it hard to accept that he loved her too. I didn't see it then (how could I have?) but she was his creation also. She belonged to him as much as she did to me. You have to remember that. For all his actions and the revulsion you might feel at hearing them, you have to remember that he always believed his motives to be pure. It wasn't vengeance or hatred or fear that drove him, though all these had a part to play. It was love.

When the sun rose the next morning we could see the heavy swell battering the coast and foaming against the small outcrops of granite which rose like smooth knuckles from the sea around us. Clonmel Island and Port Albert were lost in a turbulent expanse of white water which sent a continual low roar out to us. All along the far side of the promontory we could see enormous waves breaking against the rocks and sending sheets of water spouting into the air. We put-to off Rabbit Island, the Captain reluctant to take us further in, and I could see the higher ground seething with rabbits as if the land itself was moving like the sea.

On the mainland, Sealer's Cove was closed by a rolling line of white which pitched across a narrow bar. We kept out from shore looking for an opening through and held a line parallel to the coast which took us back towards the tip of the promontory. I felt we were drifting away from her even before we'd fully got underway. The Captain pointed out a small opening through the breaking waves where a deep trough gave access to the shore. We could see the mouth of a small cove, not large enough to risk the ship, but a way in nonetheless, and we anchored in the shelter of Mt Oberon feeling the huge swells rolling beneath us towards the shore.

The whaleboats were lowered over the side. They rose and fell with each wave, threatening to splinter against the *Shamrock*'s bulk. It was a foolish way to go ashore, but it's what we did. We would have swum if necessary. The wind sang through the halyards and we could hear it moaning round the southernmost tip of the promontory.

DeVilliers ordered Warman, Dingle and McLeod into the first boat with five of the blacks at the oars and we watched them push away from us. They disappeared between huge walls of water for what seemed minutes before surfacing again on the backs of the rolling waves. The second boat was driven against the ship as we were boarding it. Its timbers shattered along one side and before we were halfway in to shore it was sitting heavy in the water. The blacks buried the oars and dragged us forward. DeVilliers and Hartnett slung the water out with a canvas sheet while I forced my weight against the broken boards.

Great waves swelled beneath us and rose like walls on either side. No sooner had one passed to shut us off from the shore than another built up behind it, hiding the ship from view. All we could see was water; green-black, translucent, alive with shadows as it breathed about us. I knew then, we couldn't go back. Dingle mumbled the rosary beneath his breath. One wave arched above us, ribbed like the inside of a cathedral. Can you imagine it, the face smooth as glass, drawing the boat towards it? Look at it. Still, but every part of it moving. See the light in it, the colour. How the wind brushes its face, threatening to tear the membranes which hold it back. The enormous volume of water. It's as though we've brought it here ourselves. Built it out of our imaginations to hang there, perfect, for that instant before it folds and roars away from us.

We nudged our way closer to shore, finding the trough between the breaking waves and working the sling in turns. Warman's boat was safe inside the cove and we held a line towards it. Closer in, the wind eased and each stroke of the oars gained more than the one before. The water in the boat was calf deep when we found the entrance to the cove and it was all we could do to keep it there. When we made the shore, half the provisions were spoiled. The *Shamrock* had already turned against the wind and the land behind us was blanketed in cloud.

We pitched camp and Dingle repaired the boat. I set out with DeVilliers and three of the blacks, Benbow and two of the Boonoorongs, towards Mt.Oberon to survey the land. The blacks were uneasy about going. They muttered gibberish about "no-good land" and held back from the granite boulders which swelled out of the ground now on either side of us like shoulders of rock. We reached the top of the first ridge and descended into a valley of burnt tea-tree.

The ground was thick with soot that rose in black clouds

as we shuffled through it. All around us were charred and twisted limbs. They rattled like bones above us in the wind. The valley had only recently been burned and every so often we saw the blackened body of a bird or native rat which had been slow to get away. Nobody spoke. The blacks seemed anxious to be out of it and kept looking to the higher land. I felt uncomfortable myself, what with the soot clagging our throats and the smell of the place.

Coming out of it we found the remains of some native huts, abandoned long ago by the look of the ground about them. I watched as our own blacks inspected them from a distance. There's no good feeling between the Gippsland blacks and ours, especially the Boonoorongs. Even Benbow seemed disturbed to find them there and steered us away from the huts towards the next ridge. By the time we reached its top a fine drizzle had begun to fall.

As far as we could see there was thick bush shrouded with rain. I'd never considered the scale of it before. For all the words in Cavenagh's paper, for all our preparations, I'd never imagined it would be so vast, so utterly inaccessible. No map could have prepared us for what we saw from the top of that ridge — our first real look at what we'd taken on. It stretched in endless folds of dark green away from us like another sea, though without the clear line of a shore for us to cling to. It offered nothing in the way of hope: no clearing, no smoke, no sign of life.

I thought of calling out for her, just to hear how small my voice would sound. How foolishly optimistic we had been. How easily deceived. To think that we could walk in and take her out of it. The blacks refused to go further. "No good land," they said, and I felt the same unease they showed. How to accommodate such a place? So still, so silent, so inconceivably huge!

De Villiers directed us back towards the cove with its narrow beach and ordered row of tents. The next day he was laid up ill. He sent Warman out with Hartnett and Lively, one of the Melbourne blacks, and told them to follow the coast around then strike inland on the far side of a line of hills we could see from the camp. Warman strode determinedly along the beach, oblivious to the rain, with his eyes set firmly on the horizon while Hartnett and Lively trotted along behind. We repacked the dry provisions into the boat and waited for the swell to abate.

The cloud lifted from the coast and we could see the long, straight line of a white beach stretching from Port Albert to the horizon. Somewhere along it she had come ashore. Somewhere, I believed, if we could find the spot, there'd be signs directing us to her: the remains of a boat in the shifting dunes, initials carved into a tree, clothing, perhaps the figurehead from the foundered ship, the shape of the woman herself pointing blindly into the endless miles of scrub. Even then, I believed that such a thing existed. I believed we'd find it. Faith, you see. I still had faith in her.

When Warman returned he told of how they'd come to a great stretch of low-lying land that ran between the end of the promontory and the mainland like a sandy bridge. Along one side was an open shallow inlet with miles of sand exposed at low tide. Hartnett found the remains of another native camp and, much to Warman's disgust, set about sketching it and scouring the ground around it. He picked up small stones and bits of wood and slipped them surreptitiously into his pockets, thinking Warman couldn't see. Later I saw him scrutinising them inside his tent, measuring, scribbling notes into his book.

Warman had left him scratching in the dirt and had set out to cross the sandy bridge alone. He'd pushed through stunted scrub for a mile or so before turning back to find Hartnett still squatting where he'd left him. Lively was further back, sitting in the shade. Apart from the camp they saw no other sign of blacks. Warman said the whole thing was a waste of time. That night we set a watch against the empty land and we were anxious to be gone.

The next day DeVilliers was still unwell. It seemed the place affected him. That, or the thought of facing her at last. The closer we got to her, the more unsettled he became. You've seen the accusations: malingering at the lakes; spoiling the blacks. Sometimes I wondered if he wanted her at all.

Cavenagh liked him well enough. But then, he was what the papers needed. Philanthropic. Morally sound, or so they had us believe. Even his name was right: Christian J. DeVilliers. A Christian leading us into the wilderness! Cavenagh knew how to construct a story. They followed every step we made in Melbourne. Their happy band of bold adventurers! It would have been disappointing if we'd landed easily. I wondered if Cavenagh hadn't brought up the sea himself just to pit us against it. Good men against the elements. A story needs suspense.

The swell was still up the following morning when we left the relative safety of our cove for Port Albert. More of the stores were spoiled. We found the entrance late in the afternoon and landed on Snake Island. DeVilliers distributed the rations and we looked across the narrow stretch of water to the waiting land, anxious to make a start.

That night we could see the small specks of the blacks' fires along the coast and back towards the ranges. At times they seemed so close I felt I could reach out and hold them. I could almost feel their warmth. Later in the night they appeared to shift, blinking out and reappearing closer or further away. The clouds cleared above us and it seemed the night was filled with small specks of light separated from us by a huge expanse of black.

There were few believers in Port Albert. Things were worse there than they'd been in Melbourne. "Do-gooders" they called us, as though they'd lost all faith in goodness. The further out we went the worse it got. Christian men cohabiting with blacks. The law replaced with secrecy and guns. They sneered at us and sent us on our way, unmoved by the plight of one of their own, unwilling to offer their assistance. You see how bad things were, how important it was to find her. There was a man who kept his sugar in the skull cap of a black. There were rivers choked with bones. At times I feared they might turn their guns on us.

I can see now how they feared us as much as we did them. Inexperienced. Poorly equipped. Dragging our boats behind us on borrowed drays. We were hardly an impressive force. Left alone we might have perished in the bush. But we were witnesses you see. It was Cavenagh who gave us power. True, there were those who wished to join us in the search. Hunters like your father. They came to us with loaded carbines slung across their shoulders, their eyes dancing at the prospect of setting out against the blacks. Only when DeVilliers sent them on their way did they see how much of a threat we were. They eyed us then with the suspicion normally reserved for missionaries and priests. Misguided zealots, they saw us as.

Meddlers. Too self-consumed to see what difficulties we faced. They couldn't understand what drove us.

Your father might well have been among them. He had the same uncomplicated view of things, the same firm-footed, misguided confidence that came from never being questioned. In the early days he spoke of places like Boney Point and Butcher's Ridge as if he knew the stories behind their names, and showed no shame at it, no sense that anyone would see what happened there differently to him.

It gave them strength, this ignorance of theirs. They built on it, propped it up with stories, protected it with ridicule and lies. It was like a fire they stoked, fanning it into flames whenever the need arose. How it burned for us! I must admit, there were times I envied them their carelessness, their back-slapping camaraderie; times when I longed to join them. You see how fear can give a people strength. The common enemy. I shouldn't scoff; it's made us what we are.

DeVilliers borrowed drays from Tara Ville, one for each of the boats, and we set off through the bush towards the lakes. Can you see us, heading inland with the roar of the sea behind us, the boats laden with stores and trinkets for the blacks — fish-hooks, nets, shining knives — and the land rising and falling before us in endless undulations? DeVilliers climbed to the bow of the first boat and rode there for a time, peering into the tangle of scrub before him as though looking for a landfall. It wasn't easy going. The blacks pitched their shoulders against the drays to keep them moving, easing them over gullies and roots and straining against the weight of them.

We forged our way through great forests of mountain ash which towered above us, the green canopy hundreds of feet above our heads with the sun coming through it in thin lines.

Everything was awash with a strange green light. Small birds flitted in front of us and we could hear their whip-calls from deep in the forest; that and the constant dripping of water. The ground was wet beneath our feet and at times the drays sank into it almost to their axles.

DeVilliers was more composed now, with the mockery of Port Albert behind us. He appeared to have recovered his sense of purpose and guided us confidently towards the lakes which shone before us now with the promise of her. For all the hardship we faced, there was the sense that we were moving closer to her. I remember looking up at DeVilliers, standing in the bow of the first boat with his silver watch and his carbine by his side, and feeling a newfound admiration for him; a confidence that, despite my earlier reservations, he was the only one who could lead us to her.

The others must have felt it too. Warman strode purposefully through the bush, pushing the giant fronds of tree-ferns aside and cutting saplings where they hindered the path of the boats. Hartnett and McLeod drove the bullocks on. The movement kept our spirits up. Each slow step, each rotation of the wheels took us closer to her. We were certain of it. All it would take was time. Even Dingle, who had found the going hard at first, seemed to draw strength from the forward movement.

At Neale's station we had our first real intelligence of her. All of our hopes seemed justified; to be so close to her so soon! Imagine our excitement; the sense of achievement we felt at the end of our first day out when we received the news of a marked tree less than a day's journey further on.

Thomas Francis, a settler who'd taken up a run not far from Mr Neale's, brought the information to us. He'd seen the tree with his own eyes; stumbled across it by accident he claimed, though I felt certain it was fate that brought him to it. A native cherry marked with her own hand! The initials "H.B." cut clearly into its trunk. There was no doubt in my mind that it was her. How else to explain its presence there — a clear sign of intelligence in the incomprehensible bush?

I would have left that night to find it if DeVilliers hadn't insisted that we rest. Exhausted as I was, my hands stinging from the cuts of sword-grass, I would have turned the drays around myself just to sleep close to it, to feel the cuts in the soft wood with my own hands and trace my fingers through them. The more he spoke of it the more enamoured I became. "H.B." How much rode on such simple marks! Childlike, he said they were. And the tree shimmering with light as the sun went down behind it. One tree in what seemed an endlessness of trees.

But Francis refused to take us to it. Mistrust, or spite, or sheer pig-headedness — something held him back. Fear, perhaps, of the implications of his find, the ridicule and accusations of siding with us, of being seen to be a believer. There were bonds, you see, which held these men to each other in a way we could never understand. Whatever it was that made him act the way he did, there was nothing we could do. The rain set in that night and he refused to budge. Instead, he indicated with a vague wave of his arm the direction the tree was in and we could do nothing but wait. The rain fell in torrents. It swept in from across the mountains and filled the gullies with swirling foam. Looking out from Neale's hut, it was like a wall of water closing us off from our first communication with her.

DeVilliers pandered to him, offering every manner of assistance if he would lead us to it, and when that didn't work we turned to threats: exposure in the papers, official reports. I thought of turning my gun on him. (See what she had done to me? How far I'd come?) But he kept staring into the dark immensity of the bush and we were powerless against it. Even if he'd agreed, there was still the rain. I imagined her out there in it; half-naked, sheltering beneath slabs of bark around a sputtering fire. I imagined her sleeping on the wet earth, listening to the hopeless sound of rain and mustering the strength each night to fend her captors off, fighting to keep herself pure. Such fortitude, such virtue. To resist the natural urge to draw warmth from the body which lay beside her! My faith in her was complete.

It would have been foolish for us to leave in those conditions. I took to using my own knife against blocks of wood from Neale's pile, sliding the blade beneath the bark to carve out the same rough shapes as she had made. And it wasn't until the letters took shape before my eyes that I realised I was doing it. Francis caught me at it once, skulking around in the half-dark for firewood and sniggering across my shoulder. It was all I could do to restrain myself from sinking the blade into his own soft flesh. But where would that have got us? We needed him.

For two days we stayed there waiting for the rain to stop, getting on each others' nerves. DeVilliers was content to sit it out. I wondered again at the strength of his commitment then, when with each hour she moved further away from us again. Francis spoke about the tree at length: teasing us with descriptions of it; hinting at its location (beside a creek, about twelve miles out from Tara Ville); recounting how he stumbled onto it as if it was the easiest thing in the world to find. He planted it in our imaginations and watched it grow. And all along, I knew he was laughing at us, stringing us along. It crossed my mind that he might have made the whole thing up, just to see how much we'd swallow. But again, consider our position. What could we do but take him at his word? The tree, at least, offered us some hope.

Eventually, the rain let up enough for us to leave Neale's. The earth was wet beneath our feet and great clods of it stuck to our boots and caked the wheels of the dray. Francis agreed, under some duress, to take us to the tree. To continue to refuse, with the rain clearing and no legitimate excuse at hand ... I mean, what else could he have done?

Surprisingly, DeVilliers decided not to go with him. Instead he stayed with the boats and guided them towards the Glengarry. Nine hours it took them to traverse a half-mile of swamp ... neither the boats nor drays completely suited to the task. I would have thought he'd have wanted to see the cherry for himself.

I went with Warman and Francis and two of the blacks to find it. Francis rode while we trudged along behind. No doubt he enjoyed the sense of power it gave him. He could have led us anywhere he wished, or bolted into the bush, leaving us to retrace our steps with no hope of finding the tree ourselves. We passed through great forests of stringy-bark and blackbutt as we approached the ranges, the bark hanging like strips of flayed skin from limbs eighty feet above our heads. When we stopped to rest our legs we heard the scratching of animals in the undergrowth and the unnerving mimicry of lyrebirds deep inside the forest: the "thock" of axes against trees, dull sounds like shattering bone followed by low, drawn-out wails of mock grief and the sharp discharge of carbines. A whole

27

repertoire of stolen sounds echoing through the still bush as if the birds bore witness to some horrifying massacre.

Francis tended his horse as though he hadn't heard a thing, or as if the sounds were so commonplace as not to warrant comment. The blacks were visibly shaken by them. They rose from where they squatted on their haunches and looked nervously about, all but ready to flee. I was anxious to be moving too, to hear the comforting tread of our own feet against the bracken and the regular breathing of Francis's horse. But it was Warman who seemed most disturbed. He reached for his gun and stood, ready to confront whatever it was that might issue from the bush. With each new sound he turned on his heel, swinging the gun before him. And the awful thing was, there was nothing he *could* confront. Nothing solid took shape before him. He wanted something he could grab hold of and shake or strike his fist against, and the longer the source of the noise eluded him, the more distracted he became. He fired a shot in the air and it echoed back at him, part of the general din. Francis looked at him then, more bemused than surprised at what he saw. The sounds continued for perhaps five minutes then slowly died away. The last mournful wail was like a woman crying a long way off and, after that, the bush was strangely quiet.

The episode wasn't mentioned again and if it wasn't for the faint smell of powder and hot metal from Warman's gun, it might never have happened. Francis, it seemed, was practised in denial, and Warman was loath to acknowledge his fear. I said nothing and it seemed we both understood the incident would never be raised again. It wasn't so much lies that shaped our accounts of what went on out there as silence.

Mid-afternoon we came across a creek that we followed

along for about a mile before Francis pulled up his horse. There was a tree further along the bank and even before he pointed it out, I knew it was the one we sought. The shape of it matched the image Francis had etched firmly in my mind. Even now I can still see it as if it's there, growing before my eyes. The wet leaves shone like bits of glass in the wind and I could barely bring myself to approach it. Later, we'd find the remains of mia-mias in a clearing and a number of other trees marked with an axe, but to my mind they were as nothing against her tree.

Warman approached it first. I saw him reach out to touch the markings on the far side of it and nod as if to confirm what Francis had already told us. Imagine my surprise then when I looked myself (approaching as one might approach an altar) and found not only that, but more. "H.B." as clearly cut as Francis had said it was and, beneath it, the childish picture of a sloop. A boat fifteen miles from the coast! And beneath the sloop, the letters "BRIT" carved in the same clear hand.

We inspected it from every angle, dancing around it like moths about a flame. "BRIT". *Britomart. Britannia!* Britannia and everything she stood for. Such joy! What could the sceptics offer now, those who would have let her rot? I was moved almost to tears by the sight of the tree and the sweet fragrance of its leaves. The place around it was remarkably still, and quiet. The wind dropped to little more than a breeze and, when we spoke, we found our own voices came out like whispers, so huge was the silence that surrounded us.

It was Warman who suggested that we cut it down. The thought appalled me. At first I thought it was some kind of joke, a failed attempt at humour. But I saw the set of his face, the authoritative glare he gave us, and knew that he would do it. The brutality of it! The vandalism. Not just to destroy it (this was secondary, you see); what he wanted was to own it. To possess it in the cheap, insubstantial way that you might possess a pair of shoes, or a painting done by someone else. It was a prize ... something to be carried out and displayed as proof of his achievement. No, a souvenir. How he robbed it of its value.

I saw Francis reach for the bow saw he had strapped to his horse's side and draw it out of its leather sheath. I would rather have felt its teeth bite into my own thick flesh than see it used against the tree. I told them as much. I even held my hand against the cold metal to restrain them. But it was useless. Warman would see it done. The tree would be his. It had taken on a new importance for him, as though it had become the object of our search. Such delusion. Such belligerent refusal to see things as they were!

The first cut was made with long and easy strokes of the saw. Francis worked one end of it, flexing to the task with obvious enjoyment, while Warman thrust and pulled at the other. Between them they set up a rhythm which sent the blade deep into the soft wood of the tree. Sap bled from the straight cut, a bright red, viscous discharge which coated the saw and dripped heavily to the ground. When they were done, their hands were stained with it.

You think I make more of it than there was. Embellishment? Contrivance? The metaphor pushed too far? I tell you, it looked like blood. I can only tell it as I saw.

The tree fell heavily. Its smaller branches shattered with its weight and the leaves, still wet from the rain, flew in all directions like shards of glass. They bent to it again, starting on the second cut while it still trembled on the ground. And after that, a third, so they had two logs of equal length — one with the carved letters (somehow diminished by what they'd done), the other to counter its weight as it was strapped to the side of Francis's horse.

You may remember it. The log was still a popular curio long after we returned from our expedition — our hunt. The last I knew it was displayed in the Mechanics Institution in Melbourne. A museum piece. It may still be there gathering dust. But what a commotion it made when it first arrived! Francis conveyed it to the Customs House in Port Albert. Yes, Francis. I watched him walk away from us in sole possession of the tree. From there it was brought by ship to Melbourne, paraded through the streets, displayed at the newspaper offices like a sideshow spectacle.

Cavenagh, you see. Generating interest. Getting the readers in. And they came. How could they not? It had a natural attraction. They came in droves to crowd around it, stand close to it, offer up their prayers. It was like a splinter of the cross in a French cathedral. Look, I've kept the cuttings. See what they said.

"A most interesting relic. The log may be seen today at our offices. It is believed 'H.B.' may stand for Henry Bowman, one of the poor souls aboard the lost 'Britannia'. We can only surmise what fate they suffered."

Surmise. Supposition. Suspense. That's what it was all about. Cavenagh knew his work, I'll grant him that. Henry Bowman! Cavenagh had his stories to tell. I'll stick to mine.

We made our way to the foot of the ranges, convinced that we were on to her. The blacks assured us her party was ahead and I believed we'd rescue her, Warman and myself, while DeVilliers was still busy with the boats. I rehearsed the scene in my mind, over and over as we walked: the astonished disbelief on her face, the slow realisation that it was true, that we'd finally come for her, then the immense relief, the gratitude, the reaching out for us. And we'd go to her and claim her as our own.

I'd heard the sacrilege of LaTrobe, *the ties and affections* she may have formed with her captors, the doubts expressed about her wanting to be saved. But I saw none of this. No doubts. No reservations. She wanted us. She longed for us to take her. I put my arms around her, pulled her gently towards me to shield her from any further degradation she might expect from the hands of men.

I dwelt on this, played it through slowly in my mind: the way her body trembled against me, her quick breaths, the short, sharp sobs, her eyes beseeching me to protect her. So vulnerable. So utterly dependent on us. Sometimes I'd vary it — alter the setting or send her captors skulking off into the bush, or hold her more closely, more tenderly. Or else we'd find her half naked, exposed in the most intimate way, and I'd wrap my own coat around her to shelter her. These were the scenes I lingered over, building on each detail, teasing out the strands of story until they shone, more real than the stands of gums we walked through.

See how it comes to life even as I talk; how it answers to our desires. It is approaching dusk when we come across her. There is a clearing, a small stream, a circle of rough huts, perhaps a tree fallen across our path and the light slanting through thin smoke above it all. You see it as a tableau. We skirt around the edges of the camp listening to their babble, watching them scrape their wretched food out of the coals, and all the while we can see her hunched in the farthest hut, oblivious to our presence. When the time is right we burst into the midst of them like demons, send them fleeing into the bush wide-eyed at the sight of us. Or there might be some resistance; a show of strength or a spear flung back in panic.

You see what power we have now, how easily things are altered. Once I had them drive her into the scrub before them and we took pursuit, discharged our carbines above their heads, wrested her away from them. Always there was the unspoken bond between us — beyond gratitude, beyond relief — a quiet acknowledgment that she always believed I'd come.

We walked for most of the day towards the ranges, rarely speaking, unwilling to interrupt our reveries except to point out some telling detail in the trail we followed. We barely acknowledged that we hadn't found her yet. Then, when we least expected it, the tracks turned towards the promontory again. Back to the coast. Away from DeVilliers. Away from the boats. Away from our only source of rations.

You see the predicament we were in? A day's food left between us; no guarantee the trail would lead to her. It was like a test of faith. And in the end we failed it, failed her. We turned back the way we'd come, feeling the gap between us widen with each self-recriminating step, then headed across country towards Bunting's Inn. Already the stories were taking shape inside our heads: how close we'd come; how right we were to act the way we did; how foolish to have done otherwise. And before long we were striding confidently towards the Glengarry, the boats, the shining lakes, convinced we'd find her there.

3

You think we were deluded? You think I've made the whole thing up? I'm not a fool you know. I can see the half-formed smile twitching at your lips, the smirk. I can see what you're thinking: the poor deluded fools, snapping at shadows, chasing their tails like dogs sniffing their own scents. Yes, your face betrays you. But you're not as knowing as you'd like to think. Not yet. Leave if you think you've heard it all before. That's right, go. I won't be disappointed. But remember, you came to me, I didn't come to you.

Don't think I feel the need to speak. Not now. I know the story well enough. I can call it up whenever I feel the need, lay it out in front of me like a piece of cloth and smooth it out, iron out the flaws. Or I can fold it tight into itself and lodge it like a small, hard stone in the back of my mind. But you, you've come here with a purpose. You want to hear. You need it. You're the one doing the chasing now. Isn't that true? Ask yourself what you're doing here, sitting in the cold listening to an old man talk about the past. You're not in a position to judge, or smirk.

There must be better things for a man your age to do, better attractions. You have a wife? A child? Or there are places you can go. You seem surprised. I'm not so old as not to get the itch sometimes. What keeps you here? The company? Sympathy for an old man who's had his time? No, I don't think so. It's curiosity. The urge to know. You feel it, don't you? The story's what keeps you here. It's like that same hard stone rubbing against your heel inside your boot. Tell me if I'm wrong. Open your mouth and laugh.

And, of course, there's her. Yes, I can see how easily she could draw you away from your wife; how other women must pale beside her. I know how all-consuming she can be, how totally dependent you become. Oh yes, I know how she satisfies desire, how she fulfils your need for affection, for reassurance. Yes, how quickly things turn around. You think you're in control then before you know it you've given yourself to her and it's as though you can't live without her. You've always needed her and it's difficult to imagine she *isn't* there.

Will I tell you more? Should I bring her to life again before your eyes? You see who holds the power now? Perhaps I should send you home, crawling back to your wife and child who couldn't hope to satisfy you now. Or I could draw it out, keep you sitting here all night waiting for a glimpse of her and twitching with anticipation while the cold creeps further inside your bones.

Yes, I've learnt from Cavenagh. I know his tricks. I can build suspense. I can hold you where I want you, play with you for a while, watch you squirm with the need to know. I can draw the tension so tight you'll feel it like a physical thing — an itch or a sharp stick being turned against your back. Don't think you're in a position to smirk. Not now.

You think we went in there blind to the way things really were. We'd heard the stories the same as everybody else: Ronald Macalister dragged off his horse by blacks, his head disfigured beyond recognition; Clutterbrick murdered at the Heart; the settler speared outside his hut, so many spears in him he couldn't fall down. We'd heard of the double murder at Loughman's, the horrible discovery of the shepherds' bodies. Yes, we'd heard it all: the sickening accounts of corpses baked and eaten; of blacks dragging their dead behind them from camp to camp.

And for a while, we believed them all — believed they were simple acts of savagery, unprovoked attacks, wanton depravity. The blacks were charged with an insatiable lust for blood. Savages, brutes, the very opposite of what we are ourselves. You see, it was easy to believe. In a way, the stories reassured us. Oh yes, we felt anger, disgust, the urge for retribution, even grief (as though the loss was our own), but underneath it all there was the satisfaction of having our fears confirmed. They were beyond civilisation, beyond goodness. There was nothing we could do.

There were other stories though — not fully told or fully admitted to — but more unsettling for that. No doubt you've heard of them. They still linger after all these years, snippets of gossip, part hearsay, part conjecture, but always with the possibility of truth behind them; things about ourselves so far outside the realm of acceptability we couldn't hope to face them. They didn't reach the papers. Instead, they ran like a dark, heretical undercurrent beneath us. And we edged around them, not daring to test how deep they ran.

"The Highland Brigade." "Sons of Scotland." You've heard of them? Infamy doesn't fade. You see, the stories are still being told, their feats still grow in stature. Groups of men set out against the blacks — not spontaneous eruptions of violence, but calculated, well-planned expeditions. Sorties, hunts, call them what you want. They had a purpose. There were ideas behind them. Simple barbarism would have been preferable perhaps. And there were names. Not unimportant names but men who held some clout. You'd know them if I told you.

They went well-armed: carbines, muskets, lengths of rope. All sworn to secrecy. Compatriots in arms. And they knew what they were doing. They knew the terrain: where to find the blacks, which way to drive them; the confluence of rivers, the sharp escarpments of stone which served as natural traps.

Oh yes, despite the secrecy and pacts, word still got out. Some men can't help but boast. They tally up the numbers: a dozen here, thirty at the Ridge, a score at Lindenow (a good day out). And the names: Boney Point, Butcher's Creek, Slaughterhouse; they echoed around Melbourne, resonant with cries and shots and screams, until we couldn't help but hear — soft at first like the sound of wind through trees, then building — *Massacre, Massacre,* passing from mouth to mouth in a persistent, unavoidable whisper.

You see why we had to find her? Why we had to believe? Which story would you prefer to hear; the virtuous woman lost in the bush, held by savages against her will, *left to undergo a fate worse than death itself* unless we rescue her. Or the one about ourselves? You see how attractive she becomes now, how much she justifies? You see what we'd have to face without her?

And there was evidence enough — glimpses of her between trees, the heart cut into the ground. Two native troopers saw her once, a yellow woman with red hair, dressed in an opossum cloak. They called to her but she was driven forward with a spear and, by the time the troopers had dismounted, she was lost. They found her cloak dropped in the scrub not far from where they'd seen her and from the smell of it were convinced it was a white who'd worn it.

Pack Bullock Jack had seen her too. He'd followed a party of blacks for half a day, keeping them under watch, and when they reached the boundary of his land and were forced to cross the river, he was surprised to see the hair of one of the women expand on the surface of the water like a horse's tail. By then of course, when he realised she was white, it was too late. He would have saved her long before if he had known.

You're not convinced? There was McMillan's boy. Eight or nine years old he was when he left his tribe. Chose to live a civilised existence. Learned the language. He gave a full description of her: tall, red-haired, walking with a stoop. He told how she built her hut different to the rest; how she built a small mound for a pillow. What reason would he have to lie? He'd played with her own children before he left.

There was a woman too, from this same boy's tribe. True, she had no language but she nodded when the troopers pressed her. It doesn't take much; they open up under threat. They'll tell you what you want to hear alright. It was the bag that gave her away by all accounts — made of native grass it was, but knitted in a European knit. An exact facsimile of a modern reticule, they said. You see, she couldn't deny she knew her. The truth has a way of getting out.

We joined De Villiers on the Glengarry and started two days after for the lakes, setting out before the sun was up. The river flowed freely and we gave ourselves up to it, let it carry us along with barely a movement of the oars. We watched the land slip past on either side of us, confident the water was drawing us towards her.

DeVilliers seemed unimpressed with what we told him of the tree. Instead, he focused his attention on the lakes. He'd heard at Bunting's that a group of blacks had come down along the Tambo from the mountains. There'd been no word of her, no sighting, nothing to suggest she was with them. But DeVilliers was convinced. He knew he'd find her there. And the more he spoke of it, the more certain we all became that he was right. The lakes were where we'd find her. We saw them stretched out before us like a string of beads — clear, immaculate, shimmering with light as the wind brushed over them. There could be no doubt. It was as though we'd always known she'd be there and all we had to do now was let the river take us to her.

It was still early morning when the Glengarry slowed and widened and we heard the soft beating of wings against water on either side of us. Everything was blanketed in a soft haze that the sun had yet to break through. It would be hot like the day before, and still. Our two boats moved silently through the water, the oars turned up and Warman calling out the depths from the front boat. We could see the faint shapes of trees shrouded with haze, and white birds draped like bits of rag in their twisted branches.

No one spoke. It was as though we half expected her to come floating across the water towards us. At one point we heard movement away to our right and we dipped our oars to still the boats. We sat there, midstream, for perhaps a minute or two with the water sliding past and peered into the distant bush. Nothing came. Nothing materialised out of the haze.

Then, just as we were about to turn back into the current, we saw hundreds of birds start from the trees. They rose like a dark cloud against the sky and disappeared downstream. What startled them, we couldn't say. Ourselves perhaps. Warman's exploratory voice? When they were gone, the bush closed into itself again as if some unwanted violent impulse had been discharged from it.

McLeod leaned forward and grabbed Benbow by the shoulder. He pulled him towards him and half-stood so he was staring into Benbow's face.

"What's it mean?" he demanded. Benbow looked blankly back at him, not giving McLeod the satisfaction of a response. "What's it damn well mean?"

The boat trembled beneath us and the blacks shifted their oars to steady it. De Villiers ordered McLeod back to his seat but McLeod wouldn't let it rest. He kept hold of Benbow's shoulder and I could see his fingers digging deep into his flesh.

"He knows," he said. "They all know. That's why they're so bloody quiet. We should turn back."

"Sit down," De Villiers said, this time with more authority, and McLeod loosened his grip on Benbow. Dark blue welts appeared where his hand had been.

"What is it, Benbow?" De Villiers asked.

Benbow shifted his gaze from McLeod back to the bush. "Panic, boss," he said. "No good reason."

McLeod sat down and the boat rocked gently in the water. He must have realised how foolish he'd looked, how quickly he'd revealed himself. He stared back at De Villiers trying to reclaim something of what he'd lost. I think he was surprised himself at what he'd done. Perhaps it was only then that he realised how he really felt.

"We should keep an eye on them," he said. "We should go on."

DeVilliers nodded and signalled to Warman in the other boat. We lifted oars again and drifted further downstream, alert to the possibility of being watched.

For all our eagerness to be there, our confident expectation of what we'd find, none of us was prepared for what we saw when the river eventually opened into Lake Wellington. The banks of the river fell away from us and we were faced with a stretch of water so vast it might have been the sea. Its surface was absolutely still and, in the distance, its shore broke up in fog so a series of small islands seemed to drift on top of the water. Nothing was as we'd expected. Hundreds of swans pocked the water on either side of us. Even with the light diffused through the soft haze, it still hurt our eyes to look too long across the water. It seemed we'd come to a place not filled with light but made out of light itself. We clung to the shore for fear of vanishing into it.

DeVilliers directed us towards Raymond's station near the mouth of the Avon River. If anything, the light grew more intense as we approached it. The sun cut through the haze and glared off the still surface of the lake. We could feel it hot against our backs. Raymond's was set high on a hill overlooking the water and we could see a small jetty jutting into the water beneath it. Our boats would have been visible long before we pulled them in to shore. They must have looked like dark blemishes against the sheet of light.

Before we arrived, Warman killed two swans—for food, he said, though we hardly needed it. He took aim from the front of the boat and fired towards the white centre of the lake. The light fractured before us and the shot reverberated

41

through the water, sounding off the far shore and swelling back to us. The whole lake, it seemed, shattered before our eyes.

When it settled we could see the broken bodies of the two birds half-floating in the tepid water where the surface had been rent apart. Warman directed our boat towards them and lifted them aboard. They hung grotesquely from his hands, their long necks dangling like ropes beneath them, then flopped wetly to the bottom of the boat. Behind us, a small patch of blood discoloured the water as though the lake itself was wounded.

Warman seemed to gain some satisfaction from it—taking them so easily from the lake. Making his mark. And I must admit there was a sense of power that went with it, as though the land had shrunk away from us a little at the sound of the gun and we'd reclaimed some authority over it, some surety. How easily deceived we are. To think we could start to comprehend!

You see, there was no retort from the lake or the bush surrounding it. There was no flurry of wings or sign of panic. The waters closed and settled behind the boat. Birds continued to feed. The shot might never have been fired at all. In the end, all we had were two inconsequential looking birds, too tough to eat and riddled with Warman's shot.

He believed he was in control you see. There was no self-doubt or recognition that things might be other than Cavenagh had written them: us at the centre of the story; events unfolding in response to what we did; the perspective always constant. This … then this … then this … towards our triumphant climax. It was his responsibility to act.

Your father was the same (no, I haven't forgotten why

you're here), the same limited perspective. The same compulsion to make things happen. He couldn't bear to think there might be plots unfolding without him. Fear, you see. Everything comes back to fear.

Take Raymond. They made him Police Magistrate the same year we arrived—all powerful except for Tyers, the Commissioner. Between them they were the law. Everyone was answerable to them. His house commanded a clear view across the lake. No boat could cross it without him knowing. Yet, when we arrived, there was his cannon pointed into the bush behind it. A single cannon. Can you imagine it—the fear that brought it there, the uncertainty that placed it just inside the fence? The fence itself? There were loopholes in the house as well; shutters across the windows. The nearest station was only seven miles away.

What must he have made of us? Outsiders. Sanctimonious. Writing our letters back home for the paper. How we usurped his power! We used the very defences he'd set up against him: the cannon; the hunting parties; the code of secrecy. Oh yes, there was plenty of public interest. It's no wonder they resented us, the White Woman Expedition poking their noses in. The law was clear, you see, on acts of retribution—eye for eye, life for life, that sort of thing. White for black since Myall Creek. It's a wonder the cannon wasn't turned on us. We were witnesses you see, to what went on out there; to what the law had failed to deal with. For God's sake, we put it down in writing!

Raymond met us at the jetty and helped us dock the boats. No doubt he'd heard what we were there for and had been expecting us long before the Glengarry had pushed us out onto his shining lake. DeVilliers and Warman introduced themselves and Raymond led us up the hill towards his station. He was a diminutive man, too eager to please, too anxious to accommodate our needs. Warman lorded it over him, happy to see the law squirm.

He'd done his part, Raymond said, for the woman; done everything within his power to see that she was saved. And it was true, things had been done. He'd loaned his own boats to your father's party when they first set out to find her. You see, we weren't the first to take her on. Tyers had sent a party out while Cavenagh was still raising funds and forming his committee. He'd put Dana and Walsh in charge and they'd scoured the lakes and mountains for thirty-one days, driving the blacks before them. They'd come back empty-handed but they'd made their mark.

Raymond had to take responsibility for that. True, Tyers had let them loose: *"Take whatever measures necessary in my absence to secure her freedom."* But it was Raymond who fitted them out with boats and set them on their way, all guns and uniforms and good intentions. He must have watched them leave from the same spot he'd watched our slow approach. And he must have known what they were setting out to do, what licence they'd been given. *"Whatever measures necessary!"* He must have known what they were capable of doing—men like Dana and Walsh. Harpies of Hell, Warman called them, with their Native Police dressed up like soldiers in green jackets and fancy pants. They were a law to themselves.

Raymond spoke of the woman in appropriately sympathetic terms: "horrible plight", "poor wretch". He seemed genuine enough. But there were things he hedged around: what use the boats were put to; what steps the party took to bring her in; what contacts they had made. I felt he was holding something back. The more we asked the less forthcoming he became.

Of course, we know now what it was. We suspected it even before we'd made our horrible discoveries, though even now I can't be certain how much he knew and how much he guessed at. Either way he'd jumped to their defence and tried to salvage some of what he'd lost through us. Look: *"The settlers of the district have been grossly belied and slandered."* All in response to what we'd written on our return. Words. His version of the story. But words couldn't alter what we saw.

We spent the night there trying to eke more information out of him. DeVilliers asked which parts of the lake they'd searched and Raymond swept his arm in a non-committal gesture towards the top end of Lake Wellington. I wondered if he was keeping us deliberately in the dark, covering for them, or whether he knew nothing beyond the fact that his boats had disappeared in that direction. Warman pushed him about contact with the blacks. What information had been gleaned from them? How had Dana's party been received? And again there was that silence. He looked at us as though we'd overstepped our mark. Outsiders. Poking into things. Of course, I might have read him wrong. It might just as easily have been ignorance as reproach that kept him silent.

He seemed anxious to see us gone. Tyers, he said, would be at Clyde Bank in the morning, as if we were obliged to see him. The great Commissioner Tyers! But we were a private expedition. I thought for a while that DeVilliers would refuse to go. If it was up to Warman we would have turned the other way, but DeVilliers was in control and in the end he did what was expected of us. Yes, we sought approval, revealed our plans, played it by their rules. And all the time I felt we were somehow under their surveillance.

Tyers wasn't there when we arrived and I thought of Raymond's determination to pack us off and shift our focus onto someone else. No doubt he watched us go, back towards the Glengarry when all the while she was waiting for us in the opposite direction or slipping further away, back into the bush. We wasted a day at Cunningham's, unloading provisions to lighten the boats and waiting for Tyers to arrive. Cunningham was one of those self-styled Scottish lairds that made themselves at home in Gippsland, puffed up with his own importance. You would have thought we were in the Highlands from the way he'd set himself up. We shouldn't have stayed. Each hour passed more slowly than the one before and still DeVilliers insisted that we wait.

Warman and Dingle spent most of the day staring out across the lake, squinting into the light. Warman scanned the shore for signs of life while Dingle seemed more intent on the lake itself, mesmerised by the sheer size of it. He'd taken to picking up small stones like Hartnett, and leaves, and holding them up to the light. Unlike Hartnett though, who struggled to identify each one and place it in some order, Dingle was content to simply hold them, more in wonder than curiosity, then replace each one carefully where he'd found it, afraid perhaps of upsetting an order he didn't understand. He gazed into the lake with the same awestruck look of incomprehension. Here was something so bright, so still, so indefinably beautiful he couldn't hope to understand it.

Then without warning, he stood and walked toward the water. No one thought to stop him and he kept walking until the water lapped about his waist. I thought we'd lost him. I thought he'd keep on going, into the middle of it until the light enveloped him or the water closed about his head. Warman called to him, surprised at first then alarmed, but Dingle didn't turn. His eyes seemed fixed on the centre of the lake as if he could see her there, beckoning to him across the water. Then Warman started after him and I thought she *had* come to us. I thought she was really there, drawing them both towards her. But as Warman reached the water, Dingle stopped.

He stood for perhaps a minute or two, perfectly still like some creature caught in the process of surfacing from the deep, then cupped his hands and scooped a glistening arc of water across his head. He did the same again, this time bending his face to it as if to drink. There was something suppliant in it. Perhaps I make too much of it. It might be Cavenagh's influence—the desire for story—or an old man's need to tell things better than they were. Whatever, he stood there for another minute with the water dripping across his shoulders like a penitent, then turned and walked back to Cunningham's without acknowledging us.

We didn't mention it to DeVilliers. Looking at it now through the clear eyes of reason, what could we have said? It was unbearably hot. It's difficult to imagine heat now with the fire half dead and the cold already taking a grip of you, but believe me, it was hot. There was no escaping it. The shade offered little respite. Everything was absolutely still. I remember the smell of hot, dry grass and the vaporous eucalyptus haze that shimmered above the bush. And in the afternoon, when the sun was at its peak and the air itself seemed ready to ignite, Dingle strolled into the water, wet his head, and strolled back out again. The extraordinary thing about it is that it was such an ordinary thing to do. Perhaps it reflects more on Warman and myself that we were so startled by it.

The next day the lake was broken up with small waves and white-caps so it was hardly recognisable as the body of water we'd traversed the day before. Instead of translucent blue it was a dark green, mottled and ribbed with shadows where low clouds scudded over it. The spot where Dingle had stood was awash with white water and the boats trembled against their ropes as each wave dragged the sand from under them.

Dingle was up before first light. I heard the soft clicking of his beads outside my tent and knew that he was counting out the rosary with one hand while poking at the fire with the other. I dragged myself out to join him and saw him hunched forward, rocking back and forth on his haunches as a small flame flickered from the embers in front of him. If he heard me, he made no sign and it wasn't until I sat down opposite that he registered I was there.

He lifted his eyes from the fire as if I'd disturbed him from sleep and looked distractedly towards me. The beads were wrapped around the fingers of his left hand and dangled perilously close to the fire. Each one was thumbed smooth like a polished bean. A small crucifix hung from the end of them, elaborately carved with a twisted figure and studded with silver at each of its four ends. Above this was a medallion of the virgin inlaid with small blue stones. There's no doubt they were a beautiful piece of work.

I've seen plenty of prayer beads in my time, and small idols men will carry with them into the bush for protection or reassurance—missals, hymn books with hand-worked covers; one fellow I met when I first arrived had an ivory statue of the madonna with lapis-lazuli eyes—but nothing I'd seen was quite as ornate as Dingle's beads. I never felt the need for them myself, charms and amulets and the like, the trappings of belief. Dingle wore a scapula beneath his shirt as well— a dried-up piece of thong like the sinews the blacks wear round their necks when one of them has died.

I poked some burnt stubs of wood into the fire with the toe of my boot and he gathered up the cross with his spare hand. There was little warmth in the fire and, despite the heat of the previous day, a cold wind had sprung up from the south. Dingle was barefoot. He wore only a light shirt which exposed the small of his back when he leaned forward. He must have been cold but made no show of it.

I mentioned the incident at the lake, for something to say as much as to satisfy my own curiosity. He'd gone in fully clothed, you see. I mean, you'd take your boots off, wouldn't you?

"Won't be bathing today," I said, or something like that, and he looked at me as if he didn't understand. "The lake," I said. "I thought we'd lost you yesterday."

"Did you?" he said, still fiddling with the beads. "There was no cause for concern."

"I thought you'd seen her out there," I joked, trying to put him at ease, or myself at least since he hardly seemed to care if I spoke or not. "What was it you saw?"

"What was it you thought I saw?" he asked. "What did *you* see if it comes to that?"

"I saw you walk into the lake."

"And?"

"And stare at something in the distance."

"You saw something?"

"It was bright," I said. "All I saw was light. I saw you walking towards it."

"Yes," he said. "Well don't you be worrying about what I saw. It's what you see that counts; that and what you want to see. We'll find her. I believe that. Is that what you believe?"

It took me aback, the bluntness of it. It wasn't a question we'd seen fit to ask you see, not of each other. He dared me to admit to my belief ... or lack of it.

"It's what I want," I said.

"It's not a matter of what you want," he snapped, glaring at me from the other side of the fire. "Do you believe we'll find her?"

"Yes," I said. "I believe; I believe she's out there," though I don't think it was in the same dependent way that he believed—as if without her there was nothing. I don't think he could bear to contemplate that endless expanse of scrub without her somewhere in it.

"Yes," he said, "we'll find her." And he raised the medallion of the virgin to his lips and kissed it then started thumbing the beads again. He seemed satisfied to have drawn a commitment from me.

It's easy to ridicule him now. Devotion. Delusion. It has its humorous side. But at the time I envied him. You see, it wasn't only her he believed in. We'd all achieved that to some extent. It was the act of finding her that held him.

Tyers eventually arrived at seven that morning, which was just as well. Warman and McLeod were anxious to be gone. They were at the boats at first light, checking the provisions and grumbling about DeVilliers wasting time when there was a duty to perform. McLeod was worse. You would have thought DeVilliers deliberately held him back the way he carried on, cursing and kicking at the ground with the heel of his boot. There might have been something to it too; it's hard to say with DeVilliers. One thing's certain, there was no urgency to move. Who knows how long we would have stayed if Tyers and his party hadn't emerged like a caravan of officialdom from the bush to give us their blessing. I think, if they hadn't come, Warman and McLeod would have pushed the boats out from shore themselves and been gone before DeVilliers made a move.

Tyers had been doing his rounds, plodding from station to station to reassure settlers that the law was being upheld. Not that they wanted reassurance. They would have rathered they were left alone. Gippsland had a reputation, see. Settlers felt they were so far out they could do what they pleased to protect what had become theirs. And they could too. No one would have known if the law was adhered to or broken out in the uncleared blocks behind the lakes. It was hardly an issue, see. Things were done because they needed to be done. No one made a fuss. The only law was that you didn't speak.

They soon had Tyers where they wanted him. Attitudes change when men see how the law might suit their purpose. It was their law after all. Most of it was written with their property in mind. I mean, you'd be a fool to turn your back on it. They plied Tyers with tales of cattle being speared and blacks lurking about the edges of their runs, burning huts, stealing sheep. "Threatening lives and livelihood" is how they put it. Oh yes, he had a comprehensive list of grievances by the time he came to us. The law was answerable to them, see, not the other way about. They paid their taxes and expected a return.

He had his clerk, Marlay, with him and eight men from the

Border Police, all on horseback with a little cart tagging along behind. They were impressive enough: guns, licence books, court orders, satchels stuffed with papers, everything they needed to assert authority. Tyers wore a small plaid cap with gold brocade. He was a navy man by rights, more comfortable in a boat than on a horse. He'd spent two years surveying the coast up north before being lured away from the sea and here he was, traipsing the countryside collecting tax and settling disputes. He still had the look of a sailor about him though; something about the way his eyes were drawn to the lake and our loaded boats as soon as he arrived.

The clerk seemed more at home with his work. Small and neat, he was, with a waxed moustache. He set up a small table under Cunningham's verandah and brought two chairs out from inside the house. He placed them with meticulous care, one behind the table facing out across the half-cleared paddock towards the mountains, the other to one side of it exactly the same distance from the table as the first chair so whoever sat on it (which turned out to be himself) would have the use of the corner of the table and assume some of the authority it afforded. The table was placed close to the edge of the verandah so whoever approached it from the other side (which turned out to be us) would stand down looking up. It might not have been deliberate. Who can say how the mind of a commissioner's clerk works?

There was something rehearsed about his movements though, as he set the table like a waiter in a flash hotel. He laid out a sheath of bonded paper first, a day-book bound in leather, an ink-well (heavy glass), two silver seals with a block of sealing wax, a porcelain paperweight embossed with the Governor's coat of arms. Each object had its own place on the desk and I imagined him laying them out in the same deliberate way in dusty yards and by the banks of rivers from one end of Gippsland to the other. When he'd finished, he stepped back from the table to inspect his work. He was so damned pleased I half expected him to genuflect before it.

Tyers came up from the lake where he'd been inspecting our boats. He seemed bemused by our presence there, as if he couldn't quite believe we'd come. We had though, and there was nothing he could do to change it. Even the Crown Commissioner had to take us seriously! It was us he'd come to see. He asked whether we really thought we'd find her and, I remember, when Warman told him we'd do everything in our power he cast a sideways glance towards the boats.

"How well do you know the country?" he asked.

"Well enough," Warman said. "We've come this far."

"There are men who know it backwards say there's no such woman."

"And if they're wrong?"

"We've searched ourselves, you know. Dana and Walsh went out with the Native Police. And Sergeant Windridge. Each time we came back empty-handed."

Warman said nothing.

"There was no sign of her whatsoever," Tyers continued. "You should understand that. Nothing but stories. Always stories."

As if he thought we needed to be told! Never underestimate the power a story has. You're still here aren't you, sitting in the cold with no mention of your father yet? That was Tyers' mistake. He thought the stories weren't enough. How he would have liked to let her rest; the trouble she'd caused already! The things he'd had to justify! The Native Police weren't always discreet. And still the stories came. Thirty years on now and still she holds you here. Yes, your father was with them, if you haven't guessed ... with Dana and Walsh and Windridge. I know how they searched for her. I know the stories they didn't tell.

Warman still didn't speak.

"I doubt you'll fare better than men who know this country," Tyers said.

"And if we do? Whose purpose would it serve to leave?"

How much easier it would have been if he was sure. If he could have said "There's no such woman", and believed it. But that's not how he was. He couldn't shut things out.

"And if we've found signs of her already?" Warman asked. "What would be the official response to that?"

It caught him by surprise. "What signs?" he asked, as if we might be out to fool him.

Warman didn't mention the tree, not then. DeVilliers would have told him everything, but Warman held back to see what Tyers would do. "What about McMillan?" he asked instead. "Doesn't he know the country well enough?"

You see, it was McMillan who found the first signs of her. It was his story that started all the rest. The great laird himself. The discoverer of Gippsland. I mean, what could they say — he'd made it up? And where would that have left them? The whole of Gippsland founded on a lie. He wrote it down for God's sake. Sent it to the papers. Look, it's here; I've kept the whole damned lot; can recite it word for word:

We came upon a camp of twenty-five black natives ... Yes, it comes easier to me than the Lord's Prayer now. Read it, tell me if I'm wrong ... *chiefly women, who all ran away on our near approach, leaving everything they had behind them except some of their spears* ... It's right, isn't it? Word for word after all these years ... *We then searched their camp* ... Yes, they searched the camp. Imagine how I felt when I read it first ... *where we found European articles as underneath described* ... Yes? I know them each in turn. ... *several check shirts, cord and moleskin trousers, all besmeared with human blood; one German frock; two pea-jackets, new brown macin-tosh cloak also stained with blood* ... Notice how the blood repeats itself ... *several pieces of women's wearing apparel, namely, prints and merinos; a large lock of brown hair, evidently that of a European woman; one child's white frock with brown velvet band, five hand towels, one of which was marked R. Jamieson No.12, one blue silk purse, silver tassels and slides, containing seven shillings and sixpence British money, one woman's thimble, two large parcels of silk sewing thread, various colours, ten new English blankets perfectly clean, shoemakers' awls, bees' wax, blacksmith's pinchers and cold chisel, one bridle bit, which had been recently used, as the grass was quite fresh on it, the tube of a thermometer, broken looking-glass, bottles of all descriptions, two of which had castor oil in them, one sealskin cap, one musket and some shot, one broad tomahawk, some London, Glasgow and Ab-erdeen newspapers, printed in 1837 and 1838. One pewter two-gallon measure, one ditto handbasin, one large tin camp kettle, two children's copy books, one Bible printed in Edin-burgh, June 1838, one set of National Loan Fund regulations, respecting policies of life insurance, and blank forms of medical man's certificate for effecting the same* ... The holy books, you see. Everything's accounted for: the oil, the ves-sels for pouring water. Read on, there's more. *Enclosed in three kangaroo skin bags we found the dead body of a male*

child about two-years old, which Dr Arbuckle carefully exam-
ined professionally, and discovered beyond doubt its being of
European parents … Beyond doubt, he wrote. McMillan's
own words, the great man's testament … *parts of the skin*
were perfectly white, not being in the least discoloured. We
observed the men with shipped spears driving before them the
women, one of whom we noticed constantly looking behind
her, at us, a circumstance which did not strike us much at the
time, but on examining the marks and figures about the largest
of the native huts we were immediately impressed with the
belief that the unfortunate female is a European—a captive of
these ruthless savages.

You see what I mean. There could be no doubt. The
Glasgow papers nonetheless. A Bible printed in Edinburgh.
Not just children's books but the child himself. *Parts of the*
skin were perfectly white, not being in the least discoloured.
Yes, I've read it often enough. Such purity. All the elements
of her story are there. The blood. The broken glass. You can
almost see her face staring back at you, pleading for your help.
The pity of it all. How it tugs at the heart. McMillan knew his
art all right. "A *melancholy catastrophe*" he called it. Did you
read? *We have no doubt whatever but a dreadful massacre of*
Europeans, men, women and children, has been perpetrated
by the aborigines in the immediate vicinity of the spot … You
see where his story leads, what licence it would have given
him? You have to ask, would a man like McMillan make it
up?

Tyers wouldn't be drawn but he wanted to know what it
was we'd found.

"I need to be kept informed," he said, moving towards the

table with Marlay following like a shadow. "As Crown Commissioner, I must be told of new developments."

Marlay was already reaching for the ink, edging towards the chair. Only protocol kept him on his feet. He couldn't sit before Tyers, you see, and Tyers kept facing the other way.

"I have the Governor's power invested in me," he said.

Marlay was half in a sitting position, his knees bent beneath the table, his backside inches from the chair. All he needed was a little push, or one of us to pull the chair from under him. I would have done it too if I'd had the chance. I've no time for desk men. What was it you said you do? Tyers wasn't much better. He went scuttling for his books the minute Warman spoke, pulling his cap down squarely on his head as he went.

"It was one of the settlers took us," Warman said, "back along the river a way. There was evidence enough … a camp, some carving on a tree."

"And you saw it?" Tyers asked. He opened his day book and Marlay handed him a pen. "This tree. You're convinced it was her who marked it?" The ink flowed smoothly onto the paper, looping in fancy copperplate as he wrote the date, the time, the names of each of us in a column down the left-hand side of the page; starting with DeVilliers and finishing with "five Western Port blacks," putting us each officially in our place. "You couldn't have been mistaken?"

"I saw it," Warman said.

"I'll need the exact location; a description of the site. It's easy to make mistakes out here." Marlay nodded and made his own notes in a smaller book. "You'd be surprised. People lose track of days, think north is south, see things that defy description. Newcomers have a great capacity for self-deception."

"I know what it was I saw." Warman was looking at Marlay who had a self-satisfied smirk on his face now he was behind his table.

"Then you'll be able to direct us to it." Tyers unfurled a map and spread it out on the table. The line of the Glengarry snaked its way across the paper to where the lakes swelled like blisters along the coast. "Along the river you say?"

"You'll not find it," Warman said.

"Yet you did?"

"It's on its way to Melbourne with DeVilliers' letters and my report. No doubt you'll read it in the papers. You get the Melbourne papers?"

"For what they're worth. You should be careful what you write — make sure you have things straight. There was a story years ago," he said, "about your woman. A settler out along the Tambo found her. Lived with her as his wife by all accounts. It was common knowledge."

He pushed the day-book across to Marlay who blotted the page and closed it. It was Tyers' way of dismissing us, or our story at least, as if it was of no consequence at all. Marlay barely looked at us as he packed the book away like the officious little clerk he was.

"Men had seen her," Tyers continued. "Anderson who ran the Port Albert store took an order for a lady's dress. Floral with long sleeves and a buttoned waist. Two shepherds saw her strolling by the river with a book. Word soon got round. There were flowers planted in a garden. Music. She was happy by all accounts.

"There'd been no struggle with the blacks. The man had simply found her wandering in the bush and led her home. They kept to themselves, satisfied each other's needs so fully, it seemed, they had no need of further company. Under-standable after the years of solitude she'd endured.

"We arrived there, at Mace's lease in the heat of summer after following the Tambo up on a day so hot I thought the horses would drop. It was true; there were flowers in the garden — forget-me-nots, some wilted foxgloves, a wild rose tangled through the gate. I have to admit, I felt an unexpected sense of elation when I saw them. Strange how a thing so simple as a well-tended plot of earth or a square of linen flapping on a line between two trees can stir the blood and cause the heart to jump. I hadn't realised how long I'd been without the company of women. It isn't natural, you know, this constant self-denial; the things it drives men to."

He seemed for a minute to have forgotten where he was — forgotten Marlay and the day-book, forgotten Warman and me standing before the table, forgotten his reason for travelling to see us. I think it was himself as much as the settler out along the Tambo he was speaking of, as if his story had become a confession in part of things he'd done or things he'd realised he was capable of doing, since he'd seen the thoughts half-formed in his own distracted mind. Believe me, I knew what he was saying. Hadn't the same thoughts swelled inside my own head, keeping me from sleep, pushing all else to the recesses of my mind until I felt I'd burst?

"We let the horses drink then tethered them by the river," he continued, "then called out to make our presence known. At first there was no sign of anyone. The door to his hut was shut. The charred remains of a side of beef lay fly-blown a little way from it. We feared the worst. I dreaded what awaited us inside the hut. There is nothing compares with the stench of rotting flesh, nothing quite so sickening as that gagging foretaste of our own mortality.

"I sent two of my blacks to do the job, preferring to avoid confronting it directly. But before they'd pushed the door ajar with their rifle butts, before they'd had time to slap their hands across their mouths, I saw her walking towards us through the bush.

"My first instinct (as yours would have been too) was to rush towards her, to draw her towards safety, but something held me back. True, she wore the floral dress Anderson had shipped from Melbourne; she carried what seemed to be a small volume in her hand as she was said to do — a missal perhaps, or verse. But there was something about her walk, something too solid and heavy-footed for the image I had of her that kept me standing where I was.

"She slouched towards us, shambling through the grass as though her feet weren't used to shoes. The dress was stretched across her shoulders and twisted out of shape, and the thought struck me that she wasn't a woman at all but Mace himself dressed in women's clothes, playing out some perverse role he'd imagined for himself to sate whatever urges the years of isolation had forged inside him. I don't know what I felt ... revulsion, pity, anger that he'd brought us so far out to witness this. I know I felt my grip tighten on my carbine. Fear, perhaps. I'd not confronted this before.

"But, you see, I was as deluded as he was himself. Things weren't as they appeared at all. Oh yes, it was delusion, but not in the way I'd first thought. Self-abuse might have been preferable to what we found.

"The woman — yes she was a woman — kept stumbling towards us. As she drew closer, I saw the paleness of her skin

— how blanched she looked, as though she'd suffered some terrible shock and the blood had drained from her. There was little expression in her face, no jubilation that she'd been found, no sign of recognition of her own, no hesitation at our unannounced presence. She stared blankly before her and kept on walking. It might have been a mask we looked at.

"And as she kept moving closer, almost stumbling into us, I saw she wasn't white at all but black. She was hideously daubed with thick white paint that matted her eyebrows and hair and flaked like scabs from her cheeks so her own dark skin showed through like bruises against the white. Her eyes were tormented by it, reddened around their edges and barely able to close. And her hands! Her wrists showed black where the sleeves of the dress rode up. Her knuckles were caked with it.

"How long she'd endured it, I couldn't say. What other tasks she'd been coerced into performing to realise his pitiful delusions, we could only guess. There was a knitted bag tied to her wrist, the filthy remains of a bonnet looped about her neck. The book she held was grubby beyond belief, as if she'd been forced to carry it with her always. You would have wept to see her. Yes, you with all your high and mighty ideals. So confident. So sure of what you're looking for! She would have made you stop and ask what good you could possibly do by coming here. Don't come to me with your stories of names carved into trees!"

Oh yes, he told a good enough story. Charged with conviction and moral purpose it was. He even had Marlay enthralled, who must have heard it a dozen times before. And you. I can see it's caught your interest. Does it change things for you? Are you appalled by what you've heard? Will you go now, satisfied you've heard the truth or something close enough to pass for it that will allow your mind to rest?

No, I thought not. There's too much of the sceptic in you. Too much curiosity. You don't like things too easily resolved. Keep ferreting, eh, and something more interesting will rear its head to distract you, something altogether more plausible or exotic. You're not shaken off the scent so easily, I can see.

It didn't deter us either. Oh yes, it had the ring of truth to it. I don't doubt Tyers believed it. Most likely it happened much the way he told, but it's what conclusions you draw that count. And Tyers had reason enough to swallow the story whole, baited line and all, without choking on the hook. Can't you see him now, writing it carefully in his day-book in that perfect copperplate of his. Or dictating it to Marlay, giving it his official stamp, the date, the time, the exact location; filing his report, making the whole thing true then closing the book on it as he would have liked to have closed his mind. "Another sad case of delusion and abuse." Enough to keep the Governor off his back. Marlay would have appreciated the neatness of it all.

But I can see you've had enough. You want to hear what happened next. You're anxious for it, aren't you? I won't bore you with Tyers — the way he clutched at straws, erecting the battered figurehead of a ship outside his hut like some graven image of her to mock us. True, there was a likeness; the bold curve of her breast, the steady gaze directed back at whoever cared to look. I could imagine Marlay lusting after it, sneaking out after dark when he'd packed his books away. All in good time though. We'll get to that.

Tyers dismissed us brusquely when he'd done. I could see

the contempt on Marlay's face, as if it was us who'd come to them, interrupting their schedule, wasting their precious time. No doubt they hoped for more from DeVilliers. Speak to the master, they would have thought. Still, we left them with something to think about. We gave them a shake alright. Oh yes, they knew we'd been there by the time we left. Warman made sure of that.

By midday, we'd travelled the length of Lake Wellington and come to the narrow opening of the strait that snaked through thick reeds to Lake Victoria. There was a whispering as we went into it. The wind strengthened and seemed to drive us in between the dry stalks to the narrow passage. I remember looking back — apprehensive perhaps at the sound of the wind — and seeing the shores of the lake close in on us, shutting off our view and concealing us even from Raymond's prying eyes. It was a strange feeling being so confined. The water barely moved but all around us the reeds twitched in the wind and what appeared to be solid land on either side of us rose and fell with the passing swell of our boats. It was all too close for my comfort.

Hartnett, who'd been taking notes along the southern shore of the lake, had packed away his books. He started each time he heard a sound until he was twitching like the reeds himself. No doubt he expected a closer contact with his precious blacks than he'd ever really hoped for. McLeod kept up a brave face in DeVilliers' boat, cocky as ever with his gun. He had something to prove to Tyers.

We tacked from one side of the channel to the other, making slow headway, uncertain of our depths and constantly deceived by the shifting banks. The wind grew stronger, buffeting us from side to side and whipping the dark water into small peaks that sprayed across our bows. DeVilliers had difficulty controlling his boat. I saw it broach and the mast thwart swing heavily past Dingle's head and splinter against the mast. The sail ripped and flapped uselessly above them like a broken wing.

We found shelter in a small cove we called Golgotha, at least it came to have that name. I can't recall if it was us who gave it or Cavenagh. It sounds like Cavenagh, playing it for what it's worth. Whatever, the name was appropriate enough.

Even as we pulled the boats ashore we could see broken bones half-submerged in the black water beneath our feet. There were more of them tangled in the scrub behind. It was like a charnel house. I'm not squeamish. I've seen human remains before. I've helped dispose of them and dug them up again when the magistrate demanded. But here, coming across them as we did. So many of them together! There was hardly a spot we could put our feet without a hand or a jaw-bone crumbling under us. Can you picture it? Can you imagine how we felt?

I remember there was a skull wedged in the fork of a tree. There were others arranged in a small pyramid beneath it like some ghastly explorer's cairn. I still see it, you know, when I least expect it, or want it. Are you familiar with dry-stone walls — the way they lock together, the way they refuse to budge. That's what it's like. It's stood against all these years, despite my efforts to be rid of it. You know yourself, there are things will stick long after everything else has gone. Or perhaps not. You're younger than I thought. Perhaps you still think it all stays with you, every regrettable detail.

I thought that once, until I found I couldn't remember the names of men I'd known not ten years earlier; or I'd wake up in my bed and make to go downstairs where my mother would be scraping out the hearth, only to find she'd been gone thirty years and the house I'd woken in was on the far side of the world. You'll see, by the time you reach my age. There's no reason to the things that stay, no pattern to it except the one we make. Write your history now if it's what you want. Memory won't hold you to it. You'll see by the time you reach my age.

Don't look so shocked. Did you really believe it unfolded as easily as that … the past fully intact, everything the way it was? No, it spares us that at least; the things that stick are hard enough.

What I remember clearly, as clearly as if it happened yesterday, is the anger I felt at seeing them spread about like that. Such savagery, I thought. Such waste. The whole crew, and passengers as well to judge from the number of bones, slaughtered without reason so far from home.

I saw them, as I still see them now when I put my mind to it, scrambling ashore from the wreckage of the *Sarah* or the *Britannia* or the *Britomart* or whatever wretched ship it was they had the misfortune to be travelling on, then setting out across the dunes into the swampy land around the lakes. I saw them, women and children as well as men, huddling together for warmth in the small cove. They heard the air breathe through the reeds. As night fell, they saw black figures moving towards them through the scrub like dark reflections of themselves. Close to exhaustion, unarmed, there was nothing they could do but pray.

I saw what happened, and straight away I ached for revenge. I would have been the first to bring a carbine down

65

across the head of the first black we came across if I'd had the chance.

The bodies, you see, some of them at least had been dismembered. And the task of stacking so many heads! I can still feel it, you know, the anger. You see how my body trembles with it. It itches to hold some heavy implement. I can still convince myself it was the blacks had done it. It would have suited Cavenagh's purpose if it was. "*British Survivors Slaughtered by Blacks*", "*Women and Children Butchered*". It would have given his story a moralistic edge. And after all, it was what his readers wanted: the gruesome details tactfully revealed, their fears confirmed, a self-righteous call for something to be done. Let's face it, it's what you would have hoped for too. Wouldn't it have been easier to take the butchery of your own people?

Because they weren't white at all, those bones. Hartnett confirmed it for us. Every one of them was black. All shot or beaten to death with heavy sticks. There was a group of them locked together like a broken cage. I remember, Hartnett prised them apart to be certain of the number and there was another one underneath ... a child this time, only all complete with nothing broken. It was folded into itself like the skeleton of a bird with its fingers curled like claws. Perfect, it was. Hartnett laid it out flat to measure and the whole thing came apart.

DeVilliers set Dingle to mending the boat while Hartnett went from one to the other of the piles of bones. What a find it was for him ... so many in the one spot and all of them compliant. He measured and sketched and weighed, and recorded the details in his book: the number of teeth they had, the width of their brows, the thickness of the skulls where the

66

bone was split. I could see him glancing sideways at our own blacks, our Boonoorongs, trying to draw comparisons, but they'd had enough of his prodding, scientific interest. They couldn't sleep without him watching, couldn't speak without him writing down their words.

It took him the best part of an hour to confirm what we'd already guessed. Not one of them was white. DeVilliers seemed unsurprised, as if he'd known what to expect long before we'd arrived. He went calmly about his business, giving orders, taking control again from Warman who couldn't accept what it was we'd found, even when Hartnett showed him where the bullets had struck home. It was as if he'd suddenly found himself on the wrong side of some line he'd always imagined was there, or worse, that the line had disappeared and he had nothing at all to hold to in the miles of scrub around him.

I know how he must have felt. I thought of turning to Tyers myself, of seeking shelter in the law at my first glimpse of its failings. I thought everything would be changed by what we'd found and waited for DeVilliers to turn the boats around or to send a despatch to Tyers. It was our responsibility, I thought.

But DeVilliers was unperturbed. He seemed intent on moving on as if there was nothing worth stopping the glorious progress of our expedition for. He took McLeod with him in the first boat and left almost immediately to explore the channel further up. McLeod was pleased to go. There was nothing to hold him at Golgotha once he knew the bones were black and there was a smug, self-satisfied smile on his face as he pushed the boat away, confident that everything was as it should have been.

I don't know what was worse. DeVilliers knew how things

stood but did nothing. McLeod believed every story he'd ever heard about the blacks and saw nothing wrong with being rid of them. He must have looked around the little cove and applauded at a job well done.

There's plenty like him, as you know — untroubled by the past, looking confidently to the future. All he wanted was to find her, and there was no point in dallying over what had gone before.

No, I don't think your father was like him. It might have been better if he was. Oh yes, he was there before us, along with Dana and Walsh, I'm certain of that now. You've probably guessed, it was his work we looked at, some of it at least. He was handy with a carbine butt, your father. Knew how to bring it sweetly down. Yes, you've got his shoulders, there's no escaping it. Give me a look at you. Can you swing an axe? Yes, there's strength there. I should set you to chopping wood to show how easily it was done. Few of them took a second blow, those skulls.

There was enough of you in him too, to know that he couldn't ignore the past. He knew history would judge him in the end. That's why he had to find her, see. That's why he joined the second expedition, because without her, there was nothing but wood and metal striking against bone and the sound of it still echoing through the years.

It took Dingle until almost dark to repair the boat. I would have rathered we were out of there more quickly but he wouldn't be hurried. Half the time he spent staring vacantly across the water as if he'd lost all interest in finding her. I offered to help but he wouldn't have it. I might as well have offered to say his rosary for him or hear his damned confession for all the response I got.

Once, when I thought he must be done, I caught him chiselling away at some piece of wood which didn't seem to be part of the boat at all. It looked like an ornamental knife or a statuette or some such thing. I only caught a glimpse of it, God knows he was quick to shove it behind the oars, but I saw it clear enough to know there was no use for it on a boat.

I didn't say anything. It would only have made things worse. I remember, I leaned my hand against his mallet and he grabbed it away from me with such force I thought he was about to strike me. I must have shied away because he laughed and brought the mallet down hard against the oarlock instead.

"Yes, you're probably right," he said. "I could have done it. It wouldn't be so hard." To strike me, he meant — to use the mallet against me. He looked past me towards the back of the cove where most of the bones were found. "We're not that different when it comes to it," he said.

But of course, he didn't do it and I doubt he could have even if he'd wanted to. I said that to him.

"It's not your work we're looking at," I said. All I wanted was for him to fix the boat. "It's not our doing."

He was looking at Hartnett, still sifting through the bones behind us. "No," he said. "It's not my work, or yours, or anyone else's who'll lay claim to it. Perhaps it didn't happen. That would be better, wouldn't it, if we forgot we ever found this place?"

He lifted the mallet again and set to work on the new thwart as if I wasn't there. It was only when I walked back towards Hartnett that the banging stopped, and I turned to see him draw his piece of wood from behind the oars and bend his shoulders to it again.

We couldn't forget it of course. Hartnett made sure of that.

Before we left, I saw him lift what looked like an undamaged skull and wrap it carefully in his shirt like a treasured piece of china. He couldn't help himself, you see, after all the measuring and sketching. It wasn't enough to have them in his books. He couldn't drag himself away without bringing something with him. And there were so many there to choose from.

No doubt he's still got it. God knows what he does with it. I've little time for science myself; the sceptical frame of mind, never taking anything as said. You know, I never once heard Hartnett say he thought we'd find her.

Dingle eventually called to us that the boat was done and we loaded the few remaining supplies back into it. We were to meet DeVilliers twelve miles downstream and we pushed hastily away from shore. I felt the dark water pulling the boat away and heard the rush of it beneath us. It should have been easy enough to leave: the wind, the current, the promise of finding her — everything seemed to help in freeing us from what we'd found. But there was something that held us, something we couldn't completely turn our backs on. Perhaps it was Hartnett's souvenir, the thought of it grinning beneath the seat. Whatever, I felt we were skulking away, hoping the water would wash us clean.

Oh yes, it was unfinished business alright. It seemed the current dragged us too quickly away from it. Even Warman kept his oar dipped longer than he normally would have and looked uncharacteristically back.

Dingle had replaced the thwart completely with a solid length of tea-tree that he'd chiselled into shape. It did the job. The sail swelled above us as we swung into the wind. The cove slipped away from us, inconsequential in the fading light. From mid-stream there was little to draw attention to it.

The cairn might easily have been made of stones. The beach curved comfortably into the water. Behind it, standing straight against the tangled scrub like a final insult, I could see what must have been the old thwart, or part of it at least, fashioned into a simple cross and planted where we'd found the child's bones.

Dingle must have seen me looking. He kept his eyes on me and swung the boat around so we tacked a long, straight line away from it, drawing our connection with the cove so taut the whole boat trembled. We'd made no attempt to bury them, you see. I mean, Christian burial … it would hardly have been right. Besides, the spades were in DeVilliers' boat.

"We will find her," Dingle said, keeping his eyes on me as Golgotha slipped finally from view. "You must believe that now."

4

It's odd how memory serves you. Or how it fails. Before you arrived here tonight, knocking surreptitiously at my door for answers to your half-formed questions, I could barely recall your father's face. Oh yes, I could conjure up the vague outline of a man if I put my mind to it (large, heavy-jowled, a solid jaw), but of course there was never any need. He belonged to his own past, you see, as much as mine. Nowadays, no doubt, you'd make a photographic print to hold it fast, the image of him as he was then, as if you had to fight against the past to keep him from slipping into where he belongs. Yes, I'm right aren't I? Memory's not enough. Tell me you haven't sat before the magic box yourself and winced at the phosphorescent flash.

Yet now, with you sitting here before me, the outline sharpens; it takes on your features, your voice, your manner of holding the hot tea to your lips. Your father is back before me. All the years between have gone and I find, yes, I do remember. I remember what he was like. I talk with confidence about the things we did. The events fall easily into place, day follows day, night follows harrowing night. I open my mouth and it all comes tumbling out as if it happened yesterday: the search for her, the first signs of your father's presence, the journey up the river ... Almost without thinking, it finds its undeniable shape.

But I worry. If it was somebody else who knocked, somebody else who walked impertinently into my shabby little room to claim association with my past, would I have just as readily recalled a different face? Would things have moulded themselves just as comfortably to accommodate a different set of features, different questions, different expectations? Would I have found myself recounting a different story about a different past? And if no one had knocked ... ?

Ah yes, I remember. I remember we camped that night further downstream where the banks had been swept clean of any evidence of a recent past. It was better that way. A clean slate. A fresh start. We met DeVilliers early the following morning. Yes, I'm certain it was morning. I remember the sun rising through a misty haze and the call of birds as DeVillier's boat slid through the water towards us. Besides, it suits my purpose to have it that way — a new day unfolding, new expectations. Anything to hold your interest.

We watched the boat draw close, the dark shape of it silhouetted against the water, and strained to see whether it carried her towards us; sitting upright in the prow perhaps, staring out across the water, or huddled behind the mast in crumpled blankets like a frightened child. But there was only DeVilliers and McLeod and the blacks they'd taken with them, driving the boat resignedly back upstream.

McLeod was quick to tell us they'd found more bones.

"All shot," he said. "Every one of them. Tidy work."

DeVilliers told us how he'd seen fires burning on the far

side of Lake Reeves, a miserable stretch of water, choked with reed, that ran between Lake Victoria and the ninety-mile beach.

"We'll head for there," he said, as if our only guides were the flickering lights seen from the far side of an unreliable stretch of water. Still, we went. What else could we do? Even as we turned the boats around, the blacks might have been moving off in their separate directions, and who was to say which light was hers?

It took us most of the day to get there. We sailed into Lake Victoria first and held close to shore, hoping to catch some sign of her. Nothing stirred but birds and the lapping wakes of our own boats. Still, McLeod kept his gun cocked. Warman, who'd been so confident before, kept his flat across his knees and gazed blankly into the wall of reeds that rose along the shore. The day seemed interminably long. Each landfall DeVilliers made seemed the same as the one before — an anonymous, scrubby point or an unremarkable hill swelling behind the reeds. The sun seemed always to be directly above us. It's strange, looking back, all the years between seem to have passed more quickly than those hours we spent drifting on Lake Victoria. And here, in the last few minutes of the day, the hands of your expensive watch have barely moved as I tell of it.

It might have been five or six in the evening — I can't be certain — when DeVilliers directed us in towards shore. It might have been later. There were birds moving towards the trees, the sun seemed less intense as I remember it. No doubt it's written down somewhere: the exact time our boats touched shore, the exact spot we tethered them like horses to a sodden log. What I remember is that we hadn't reached Lake Reeves.

We could hear the solid pounding of surf some miles off along the ninety-mile beach and could see the opening to a shallow arm off Lake Victoria where the water turned a dark blue-green and the reeds seemed thicker than they'd been before. It was uninviting, even from that distance. I doubted it was deep enough for the boats.

DeVilliers ordered us to set up camp and wait for dark. Always this holding back. Always this reluctance to confront whatever it was that waited for us round the next point, the next bend in the river, behind the next clump of trees which might separate us from her. It was as if he knew ... as long as we hadn't found her, his position was secure. *Christian DeVilliers leads the search for the lost White Woman.* It made him what he was, you see. And once we'd found her, or failed, the focus would shift to her. Or to whatever it was he knew would be revealed about ourselves.

The story was unresolved as long as we were out there, and even DeVilliers could still convince himself it would end right, with all our actions justified. He could still believe, in spite of what he knew, that we were under threat, that all we had to do was turn our backs and decency and virtue would be snatched away from us. It's not hard to imagine, is it? Even now there're people who will argue that's how it was (or is) ... that we planted civilisation here against all odds. You see them polishing their pedigrees, trying to salvage something from their families' pasts.

Yes, the past! It says something about us, don't you think, that we're so preoccupied with it? Isn't that what you're here for? Patting yourself on the back for who you are? Yes, I know your type — all ears for what you want to hear, all shock and indignation for the truth. Well listen up, we're not done yet!

DeVilliers kept the story going alright. He kept sending his instalments back " ... *be assured that if the Almighty spares my life, nothing shall be left undone to sucessfully accomplish our undertaking.*" And Cavenagh kept beating them up to hold the public's interest and put their minds at rest.

"*Mr DeVilliers announces the assistance he receives on every side from the settlers. Mr DeVilliers writes in high spirits. Mr DeVilliers speaks well of his party, both blacks and whites. Mr DeVilliers will have no difficulty in finding the object of his search.*"

Cavenagh needed a DeVilliers. And once he had him he knew how to make him work; how to flesh him out, dress him in adventurers' clothes, how to shape him into what the public wanted.

"*We assert, with confidence, our firm belief that the poor woman will be rescued.*"

If they needed her, they needed him as well. Confidence. Belief. Reassurance that something at least was being done. DeVilliers let them sleep at nights.

Look what Cavenagh gave them: "*Mr DeVilliers recently transmitted to us the happy intelligence that he has moved closer to making communication with the unfortunate woman held captive by the blacks. He reports a meeting on Lake Reeves with two blacks who he has every reason to believe were in recent contact with her. One, he writes, hummed a tune that bore a remarkable similarity to the 100th psalm and said that was what she used to sing.*"

Do you know the 100th psalm? Have you heard it sung? Yes, I'm sure you have. With full choir no doubt, and the organ heaving over it. You could probably sing it now if you put your mind to it. Yes, you look the type — the right schools, the good

Christian upbringing. Your father would have made sure of that. Staking his claim on the future, he would have said, hoping it would help obliterate his past. Oh yes, he knew how to mouth the words, your father. Don't worry, I don't want to hear you sing. I know the tune well enough. "*Of mercy and of justice my song shall be . . .*" I'm not completely ignorant. And I know the sound DeVilliers wrote about. I was there, remember. I heard it as clearly as I'd hear you now if you opened your mouth and sang.

We left around midnight. DeVilliers thought he could see lights again reflecting off the water on the far side of the lake. He might have been right. The night was filled with stars and, in places, it was hard to tell where sky gave way to water. I remember we rowed across to the shallow opening of Lake Reeves, the regular drag of our oars the only sound we could hear in the empty night except for the hollow pounding of the surf.

The further we went, the harder it was to move the boats. Lake Reeves was choked with grass. Long strands of it brushed against our keels and snagged the oars. Cavenagh would say it was like the tangled hair of a drowned woman, the way it shone and swayed beneath the surface of the water, the way it seemed to pull against us. But then, that's Cavenagh, always looking for the emotive turn of phrase. What I remember is it took us an hour or more to find an entrance through the weed and, even then, it was hard-going up the lake. It was a miserable stretch of water — shoal and practically impassable, and always the restless pounding of the surf less than a mile away.

We eventually found a way up a narrow arm where the reeds grew so close about us that it would have been difficult to turn the boats around. There was no sign of the lights DeVilliers had seen. Everything about us was still and black. We seemed to have drifted into some wretched backwater from which there was no way out, and the further up we went, the shallower it became, the closer about us the reeds grew. The air hummed with mosquito life. And still DeVilliers insisted he'd seen the lights, still we pushed the boats forwards.

When I'd all but given up hope, Dingle claimed he saw something shining through the reeds. We stopped the boats and waited, and sure enough, there was a dim glow not half a mile away that seemed to move across the water or hover over it. Then it would disappear only to appear again some hundred yards or so further on, sometimes flaring more brightly above the reeds like a beacon guiding us in to land. It moved steadily closer to us. McLeod cocked his carbine and held it ready. DeVilliers bade us all sit quiet.

We could hear a disturbance in the water, like something heavy pushing through it on the far side of the reeds. There was no wind but the reeds clicked softly against each other as if the disturbance had been transferred to them. And it reached to us as well, not as a physical thing so much, like water lapping against the boats, but as a feeling of things being drawn tight and expectant, as if one of us might suddenly cry out, or McLeod's finger might squeeze too tightly against the trigger of his gun and relieve the night of its tension.

They say you hold your breath. I expect that's what I did, though I couldn't say for certain. It's not the breathing you remember, or even the words that passed (or didn't pass) between us. It's the unnerving, heavy feeling that none of us were prepared to put a name to then. It's easier now, after so many years. I know the way it catches you by surprise when you think you've finally got the better of it. Oh yes, it comes back, believe me, when you see how many years have passed and the yawning hole at the end of it. I call it fear.

The boats sat perfectly still in the water. An hour, half an hour? Morning was still a long way off. My legs cramped, and still the light appeared and disappeared; it changed direction slightly, drifted towards the far side of the arm then floated back again as if it sensed us there. It would find us out. All we could do was wait.

Eventually it drew close enough for us to see the flames flaring through the reeds, and we could smell them too, the stink of animal fat and burning grass, and there was a low murmuring as well. The light couldn't have been more than a hundred yards away from us when I first made out the dark shapes of figures moving behind it.

There were two of them, up to their thighs in water, pushing through the reeds and mumbling to each other as they went, fishing by torchlight in the middle of the night. Spearing eels. I saw one of them plunge his spear into the water and, as they bent to it, holding the torch down low, McLeod must have seen his chance. He swung his carbine round and DeVilliers reached out to stop him, gripping the barrel and forcing it up so I thought McLeod would lose his balance and both of them would sprawl into the water. They didn't speak but there was enough disturbance for the blacks to turn towards us and hold the torch high above the reeds. They must have seen us huddled in the boats on the edge of darkness where their torchlight faded into night and wondered what sort of awful fish they'd caught, because they turned and all but ran, stumbling through the tight reeds away from us.

They dropped the torch. It hissed and sputtered for a moment before going out, then all we had was darkness and the frantic sounds of them thrashing through water for us to follow. McLeod was first out of the boat, holding his carbine high above his head. Warman followed with a length of rope. DeVilliers sent our own blacks wading through the reeds in various directions, hoping to head them off before they reached the shore. The night was filled with cries and the rush of water and we moved the boats slowly forwards, wading ourselves at times to drag them over soft banks and feeling the pull of seagrass against our legs. I can still remember how warm the water felt, and gentle.

I heard a shot fired and there was a great flapping of wings as hundreds of birds rose from among the reeds. They shadowed past us, filling the air with sighs as they beat their soft way towards the safety of higher ground. I could hear McLeod calling out to Warman. God knows how he could see to shoot. Our own blacks must have been pushing towards him even then. There were no screams; nothing to suggest anyone had been hit, just his lone voice calling, "Warman, Warman," like a hollow battle-cry.

It was when he stopped that we heard it first, the low, mournful strains of what might have been described as song. True, there was part of it sounded vaguely like an echo of the 100th psalm — the same few notes strung randomly together in a register close enough to make it sound familiar. It might even have offered comfort had everything else about that night not been so strange … but as it was … well … And perhaps that's precisely it, the strangeness of it all. Perhaps we only heard what we wanted to hear after all, to protect ourselves from … what? Or to throw up some glimmer of hope at least. How else could we have wrested song from the piteous wailing of a man who must have seen his worst fears surface from that miserable stretch of water? *Of mercy and justice my song shall be.*

DeVilliers had us push the boats softly into shore and set out himself through some scrubby bush towards the ninety-mile beach. Hartnett went with him, and Benbow who'd stayed behind when the other blacks had gone. I heard them crashing through the bush and before long they all returned, driving the two men before them. One of them kept the wailing up while the other beat his fists against his breast and mumbled something repeatedly beneath his breath.

They still had their eels with them, tied in grass bags around their waists. When they reached the boats, DeVilliers made them spill them on the ground and they writhed about our feet like snakes, blindly feeling their way towards the water. The bags were beautifully made. All grass, they were, from the bottom of the lake, finely woven into net with plaited strings. Hartnett couldn't wait to get his hands on them.

They soon realised we didn't mean to hurt them. Blankets, you know. And fish-hooks. DeVilliers poked the eels with a stick and made approving noises and the blacks quickly scooped them up to give to us. Can you imagine their relief? *The eels,* they must have thought. *They only want us for the eels.* And how foolish they must have thought us for not being able to catch them for ourselves. We were happy enough — to play the fools, I mean — so long as they told us what we wanted to hear from them.

They took us back to their camp. McLeod didn't want to go — kept looking warily behind him as we walked across the narrow tongue of land with the birds starting to come to life in the trees and, all around us, the stirring of things and the rising sun spreading a strange light across the land. I can't say I blamed McLeod for being scared. I would have felt more comfortable back with the boats myself, or safely away from shore in the open expanse of water we'd left behind. The whole place seemed too close, as if the weed that had threatened to stop the boats had somehow tangled about ourselves and was dragging us down to a place we'd never intended to go.

Oh yes, we were the ones who had captured them. We were the ones with the guns. But even the flitting of a wagtail or a finch in the stunted trees could make us jump. The surf, so close to us now, never let up its pounding. We seemed to move to it. Can you see us, driving the two men on as if we were in control, towards ... what? And following blindly behind them. You see how we exercised our power. Each tree, each small clump of grass might have concealed things we couldn't hope to know. The ground was soft beneath our feet, like sand, and it squeaked as we trudged across it, singing out its own strange music.

Eventually, we came to a place where there were two small fires smouldering in a clearing and one of the small huts they build. The fires were little more than handfuls of twigs and leaves with thin wisps of smoke rising into the still air. We stopped on the edge of the clearing and listened. Nothing moved. Nobody spoke. McLeod still had his gun and DeVilliers had had the sense to carry his as well. The place must have been midway between the dark lake and the ninety-mile beach and, though we could hear the constant hiss of water, all we could see was trees.

It was like one of the scenes I'd rehearsed so many times

in my mind: the break of day, the blacks taken by surprise, the domestic ordinariness of a group of them caught preparing food — and, on the edge of the camp, removed from the centre of proceedings, the familiar hump of saplings overlaid with bark, the dark womb swelling with the possibility, the hope, the certainty of Her concealed within it. And we would draw her out. We would go to it and reach our hands into the cool dark air and feel the softness of her flesh inside and bring her, wide-eyed and impossibly white, blinking into the light of day.

It was all there. Everything as it should have been. Except they'd gone. There was no one crouched beside the smoking fires, no scurrying into the scrub, nothing except the fires themselves to suggest they'd been there at all. And, even before we approached the hut, we knew the disappointment of miscarried hopes. The two blacks stepped into the centre of the scene — unsurprised, unhurried. They squatted comfortably by one of the fires and it was us, not them, who felt a strange unease at the lack of noise about us, the sense that there were others near, unnervingly out of sight but watching our every move. McLeod held his gun stupidly in front of him, pointing out the direction they had led us in then swinging it erratically from side to side like a compass needle searching for true north.

We stayed grouped together — security in numbers I suppose, though it wasn't planned — and watched as two figures silently materialised from among the trees and, without speaking, took their places by the other two beside the fire. And, before we knew it, there were two more, and a group of children squatting at the other fire as if they'd always been there and, for some reason, our eyes had been unable to see them. And a young boy carrying a spear. And an old woman huddled beneath a possum-skin rug. And another woman. There were twelve of them in all with the two who had brought us there. They seemed unperturbed about our presence as if the two we'd found eeling had somehow communicated with them that we meant no harm.

They welcomed us in to their fires, scraped something out of the ashes to offer us as food. The children showed an interest in our boots. McLeod must have realised how foolish he looked with the gun and rested it by his side while DeVilliers drew more fish-hooks from his pockets to present to them, as much as questions to be answered as as gifts. He wouldn't be disappointed. One of the women had spent time at Cunningham's and knew well enough what we were after. Warman only had to mention her, what with the guns still visible and the cove at Golgotha not half a day's journey away. Yes, she knew the white woman, the *Lohantuka*. She'd seen her! And suddenly the whole journey up the lake seemed inconsequential. I half expected her to walk out of the bush the way the blacks had done and greet us. Dingle crossed himself. McLeod moved towards the humpy. Just the idea of her, you see, just the thought, and it was as if she was there among us. The whole forest seemed filled with light.

"White woman plenty plenty cry," she said, and pointed to the mountains where she said she was now with a man called Bunjil-ee-nee.

Yes, Bunjil-ee-nee. You've heard of him? What a gift he was for Cavenagh. The monster he'd been looking for! What a gift he was for us. You know the stories: a giant of a man; inhuman. As strong as twenty men. Left-handed. Even the blacks were in awe of him. Two wives and still not satisfied. How Cavenagh made him work!

And not just Cavenagh. Can you imagine how we felt ourselves? Out there for close on three weeks with nothing but the purest motives, and suddenly our quest had turned into a hunt. And we were on to him! He'd fought for her, the woman said. Claimed her as a prize and taken her away into the mountains, and nothing could persuade him to bring her back.

Before she'd finished, one of the men starting humming his tune again — louder this time, insistently as if he wanted us to hear — and Dingle hummed it with him, rounding out the notes and altering its pitch until it was possible to believe ... yes, possible ... what reason did we have not to want to believe at least? And the woman told us it was Lohantuka's song. The song she used to sing before Bunjil-ee-nee dragged her away. The old 100th. The white woman's song! And here it was, issuing from his heavy lips and floating through the trees, out across the water. We could have wept to hear it. It was what we wanted, see? Answers to our questions. Belief. And we heard it. Yes, we heard it. It was a humming noise.

We spent the rest of the day and that night in the blacks' camp securing their friendship, and the following morning they agreed to guide us towards Bunjil-ee-nee as long as we agreed to offer our friendship to him in return. They were scared of him, you see. That's what we thought at least. The great Bunjil-ee-nee! He wasn't one of them, not one of the lakes blacks. He was from the mountains, and I imagined him looming disdainfully over us, keeping watch over every move we made. Yes, I could see why they'd be scared, though looking back, maybe not half as scared of him as they were of us.

They accompanied us to our boats and we set off, back up Lake Reeves, with half of them aboard and the water brimming at our sides. We took three men, two lubras and a young boy. They guided us through the reeds back to the broad waters of Lake Victoria then held us close to shore as we made for Lake King and the mouth of the Tambo.

We'd not gone far before we saw three or four canoes drifting on the water ahead of us. The shore was a tangle of dark scrub, shaded by larger trees that reached out in places across the water or had fallen partly into it. The sun glared off the lake like the water was a sheet of glass. And there, just before the line of shadow started, small pieces of the land seemed to have come adrift and floated like strips of bark on the still lake. They might have been dead logs, except that they seemed to be moving with us, keeping the same distance between us, even when we pulled the oars more swiftly. And when we looked more closely, shielding our eyes against the glare, there were more of them, shadowing us closer in so it seemed the land was moving with us as we plied our way around the lake.

One of the blacks we'd taken aboard called out to one of the canoes and made signs of friendship, and before long the water was filled with them. Their bark canoes crowded silently around us, rubbing against our heavy boats, threatening to send the water spilling over the sides. Each canoe held two or three men. Big, they were, and solidly built. They stood tall and steady on the water as they approached, barely disturbing the surface as they brushed easily across the lake. All along the shore we could see them — coming towards us, surrounding us, walling us in — until we couldn't say whether our own boats moved or not.

They spoke quietly to the men we'd taken and rubbed their hands across each others' breasts as a sign of welcome. I heard the words "Melbourne-Melbourne" and "Lohantuka" mumbled over and over as news of us passed between them. Back it went from canoe to canoe in a low murmur that seemed to rise from the water itself and fill the air around us and, before we knew it, children were being passed from hand to hand to be placed inside our boats. I remember DeVilliers fumbling in his pockets for more fish-hooks, only to find them empty and offering instead a lump of bread, three days old, from the ration box. They took it and passed it between them, each man tasting it until there was nothing left.

Eventually we saw that we'd drifted, or been taken, close in to shore without our realising it and the blacks pointed to a spot where they wanted us to land. We could hardly refuse, could we? I mean, we still had their children in our boats; there were still so many of them crowded around us. I don't know who was being held. Yes, we had the guns. We had the children. But still . . .

When we went ashore we found there were more men concealed among the trees. A hundred? Two? We couldn't say. All around us we could hear voices calling out from the scrub and the rustling of leaves. There might have been as many blacks as trees for all we knew and, after a while, the voices seemed to come from the far side of the lake as well, or perhaps from the lake itself.

Two old men gathered up all the spears and carried them into the bush, then we all sat down by the shore. Every one of them — yes, every one — told the same story. "Bunjil-ee-nee, Bunjil-ee-nee, Bunjil-ee-nee", until it became a sort of chant, investing him with more power than he already had. And they all pointed in the same direction, towards the mountains, to show where he'd taken her away. "Bunjil-ee-nee, Bunjil-ee-nee", can you hear it? Over and over again like a plea. And soon, the voices in the bush took it up. "Bunjil-ee-nee, Bunjil-ee-nee", sounding out across the lake and echoing back at us until I half expected Bunjil-ee-nee himself to come striding across it from the mountains.

We must have spent half the day with them. The children pulled at our clothes. The old men muttered "Melbourne-Melbourne," as if to distinguish us from the other whites they knew, and seemed happy that we were there. All of them knew the woman. All of them had seen her. There was no doubt in our minds. Why else would they speak of her? "Lohantuka," they said as soon as they heard it was her we'd come for. "White woman." And they pointed towards the mountains. You see how foolish Tyers had been, and Dana and Walsh with their band of harpies, the Native Police! All guns and vengeance. All they had to do was ask. That's what we thought. All they had to do was tell them what they'd come for! You see how easy it was to fool yourself out there. Of course the woman existed. It was Bunjil-ee-nee had her. It was Bunjil-ee-nee would give her up.

5

It took us the best part of three hours to reach the mouth of the Tambo with a good breeze coming up behind and the water deeper and less brackish than in Lake Victoria. Lake King was almost completely free of weed. The water was light and soft to touch and seemed to go down forever. Hartnett took to drinking it, scooping it up in handfuls and pouring it into his mouth at intervals of fifty yards or so, and each time he claimed it was better than the time before. He made notes about it in his book. He talked about the medicinal qualities of it. Magnesia. Potassium. "Purifies blood," he said. He claimed he could taste how close we were to the river's mouth from the traces in the water. And before long we could feel the flow of it beneath us as it poured out from the mountains into the lake, perfectly fresh and clear and cold when you reached your arm into it and shining in the sun like silver.

It was nothing like the water here — this dead, flat bay we've built our city on with its brown river sliding surreptitiously into it. It was alive. You could feel it. Do you swim? Do you know what it's like to plunge your whole body into living water? To feel it swirl about you? Have you felt it —

the way it takes you in and holds you? No, I thought not. You're not a swimmer. Too slow and tentative. Too careful. Yes, I know you — earth-bound. Too busy looking backwards. I never once saw your father touch water, unless it was to drink or wash.

There were great trees pushed out into the lake at the river's mouth, upended and snagged on banks of silt, with their tangled roots looming above us as we passed. Enormous things they were. Who would have thought the water could have moved them? Not one but ten or twelve of them with their great trunks shafting down through the water, draped with weed as if they were the masts of ships dredged up from the bottom of some inland sea and spat out by the Tambo on Lake King. We edged around them, overawed by the power of the river. And if it could bring them down, what else could it deliver? What else could it flush out from the mountains for us?

We eased our way into it, feeling its resistance through the boat, water straining against wood, the enormous flow of it like a tide. The banks were low. We moved through the land as if on top of it, beating upstream through country as good as any you're likely to see. Upstream. Towards the mountains. Towards Bunjil-ee-nee. And before we'd gone more than a few miles, DeVilliers turned the boats around. Yes, turned them round, and we floated back downstream again. Back to the lake. Back. The river pushed us onto it like leaves and we drifted aimlessly while the blacks conspired amongst themselves. They pointed this way then that: up into the mountains; across the lake; jabbering and laughing till it seemed the whole thing was a joke. They were playing with us. Taking us for fools. And DeVilliers was happy enough to let them. That or he lacked the drive to push the boats upstream. Too close, perhaps. Too strong a sense of purpose. Too easy to keep scouting round the lakes, close but not so close as to be compelled to act.

Eventually, they took us up the Nicholson instead. Strange how two streams can be so different. Oh, it was broad enough, and deep, but the water seemed a different colour — darker with a limey taste to it, and tepid when compared to what we'd come from. We were back among the reeds again. They blanketed the high banks and were alive with insects. Flies and mosquitoes swarmed above them, filling the hot air with noise and tormenting us, even when we kept to deeper water. There was no escape from them, unless we were to immerse ourselves in the dark river, and even then, there was no saying what swam below us or what hung suspended just beneath the surface. We slaked our thirst with it instead, trusting to Hartnett's judgment as to its medicinal qualities.

About six miles up, the reeds gave way to steep banks and limestone cliffs that towered over us. The water changed colour again — yellowish. And black in the shadow of the cliffs. At one point, where the river turned, the sunlight glared off its surface and threw our own shadows up onto the cliffs before us, huge and twisted out of shape, and we followed ourselves upstream. A mile or so further on, the river turned again and the cliffs gave way to lower-lying ground, heavily timbered but clear in parts, and the water slowed so it hardly seemed to move.

We passed the ruins of a hut with fences tumbling into the bush behind it and an acre or so of land that had once been cleared. I thought of Raymond's cannon pointed into the bush. There was a settler, you've probably heard, so many spears in him he couldn't fall down. Yes, Cavenagh again, but there was some truth in it. The further upstream you went, the harder it was to hold a lease. The forest was always just beyond the fence, and each night ... yes each night, just the thought of them ... Can you imagine it? There was a whole paddock of ring-barked trees still standing as if waiting to be cleared. Every one of them was dead. It was as if it was the trees they couldn't trust rather than what they might conceal. I remember, the door of the hut was open. There was a pair of trousers tied around a tree. We slid past quietly, keeping our eyes on the river ahead as though there was nothing to distract us.

The higher up we got, the more choices we were faced with. Tributaries entered the main stream on either side of us. Many could have taken our boats. Any one of them might have led to her ... to him. It was Bunjil-ee-nee we were after now. Things had shifted even then. Oh yes, we wanted her alright, the same as always, but it was Bunjil-ee-nee loomed largest in our minds.

Each time the river split or we passed the opening of a small creek dribbling into the larger stream, it was as if we'd missed another opportunity; and after each choice we made, the Nicholson dwindled into something less substantial than it had been before, less worthy of the hopes we placed in it. Its banks closed towards each other. Fallen trees threatened to block our way. Dead wood and tangled scrub. In places it seemed hardly larger than a creek itself with its water the colour of tea and the boats bumping over stony weirs. Eventually, we could go no further up and we set up camp with the whole thing laid out below us like a map.

The blacks we'd taken on all pointed north-north-west, further into the mountains towards the source of the Nicholson, and De Villiers prepared for a party to set out on foot next day. He seemed happy enough to follow their advice. It was McLeod who needed to be convinced. At least, it was McLeod who made a show of it. He ripped a sheet of paper from his journal and held it flat against a box then took to it with a blade. At first, I thought we'd lost him — the heat perhaps, or the whole expedition had been too much. Have you seen a man go mad? Something fails and thirty years or more might disappear. Songs and games and soiled clothes! Yes, I know how it works. Believe me, I know. When you reach my age … well … there're few surprises. You've got it all before you!

McLeod cut out paper dolls. Two of them he made. Identical in every detail, down to bonnets and pointed shoes. The paper rasped against the blade he used for shaving. And where it didn't cut, he tore it, pulling roughly with his heavy fingers until there was no doubt at all about what they were. Dolls. Identical paper dolls flapping from his hands like handkerchiefs as he walked towards the fire.

Yes, the fire. I remember he took a length of blackened wood from it and laid the dolls out on the ground. Then he rubbed the charcoal over one of them, carefully at first, gentle even, caressing the white paper as if he didn't want to tear it. He started at the head and worked down — shoulders, breasts, waist. And the more discoloured the doll became, the harder he rubbed, smearing the black stuff over it with his spit and grinding the hard point of his stick against it. The legs buckled. The disfigured torso crumpled under him. And when he'd finished, he picked it up off the ground, creased and torn as it was, and held it out to the blacks. In his other hand was the white doll — untouched, pristine — and he held that out too. Two women in the flickering light of the fire. And he demanded to know which one this Bunjil-ee-nee had. Which one was his wife? Which one were they taking us to? It was a simple enough question after we'd come so far. Yes, you know, don't you, what I'm going to say? Every one of them pointed to the white paper. And when he'd done, when he'd brought himself to take them at their word, he folded it carefully into his pocket like it was a ten pound note. The other, he tossed onto the fire.

He and Hartnett went with DeVilliers next morning. Off to the source of the river, the great Bunjil-ee-nee's retreat, armed with the last of the blankets and a shiny piece of glass. Imagine them — heading across-country, reading the land, looking for the slopes and depressions where water would flow and sit, following the trickles over stony ground, tracing them up-wards, upwards in search of the one elusive spot where a shallow pool of water brimmed then overflowed to start its slow descent towards the lakes. And all in the hope of finding him there.

They took eight blacks as well as our own, and provisions for a week. Yes, well prepared. There was a degree of expec-tation about it all. Even DeVilliers seemed committed to the task. He took three of the blacks aside, two men and a boy who belonged to Bunjil-ee-nee's tribe, and changed their names. Dingle scooped a pannikin of brown water from the river and DeVilliers poured it over them. I don't know what names they had before. They answered to whatever you called: Jacky-Jacky, One-Eye, Billy-Boy, Friday. Hartnett would have known, though he said they kept their real names to themselves. Fear, he said, of hearing them used against them. DeVilliers put a stop to that. When he'd done, after he'd called on our governor and king and waved his hands about, they were Mr Cavenagh, Dr Greeves and Mr DeVilliers himself! Yes, Mr DeVilliers. The conceit of the man, the untempered self-absorption — to replicate himself out there and bestow his name as if it was an honour. And the thing is, the poor wretch who took it on seemed pleased. He answered to it, demanded that his fellows use it to address him; he even took to following his counterpart about so, when one of our number called, not one but two heads turned simultaneously towards us.

DeVilliers himself drew great pleasure from it, as if his own self-imagining had grown out of all proportion from what he'd done. Better than naming rivers or a mountain range; better than putting his name to an undiscovered species; it was as if he'd brought himself into the world and could exercise his will twice over.

The others, the newly appointed Mr Cavenagh and Dr Greeves, were less impressed. The names must have hung on them like empty sacks. And the expectations! Who were they supposed to be? They must have limped along beside their former selves, aware that some honour had been bestowed upon them, knowing that somehow they'd been transformed. But into what? Such distinguished names. How vulnerable they must have made them feel.

They left before dawn, with the two DeVilliers stepping boldly out in front and Mr Cavenagh and Dr Greeves in charge of the stores. The following morning they were back.

They'd taken them high into the mountains — twenty miles or so over rough and broken ground, looking for watercourses in the searing heat. Then Mr DeVilliers had left them. Greeves and Cavenagh went too, followed him into the bush as if they were setting out on their own expedition, and our own DeVilliers could do nothing to bring himself back. He could have followed I suppose, but then ... He could have dragged them back ...

By all accounts he stood there, at the spot where he'd last seen them, and called his own name over and over into the bush until it was clear he wasn't coming back. Then he'd walked a little way into the scrub and stayed there, quietly, as if contemplating his own singularity for close to fifteen minutes while the rest of the blacks slipped silently away.

Abandoned. Can you imagine how he felt? Can you see him starting his slow descent back down the mountain to face us? Exhausted. Disillusioned. Frustrated at the foolish waste of time. To have watched himself simply walk away like that!

McLeod cursed himself for believing them in the first place. Even Hartnett must have lost some faith. How gullible we were! How easily led, like schoolboys prancing after them into the bush on the promise of a half-familiar tune and a cut-out doll. Giving them our own names! Don't laugh ... it's wanting to believe will do it to you. There're others have done far worse for the sake of faith.

It might have been fear made them do it. The terror of facing Bunjil-ee-nee, or of facing us when he failed to deliver. Or the names. Yes, they might well have slunk pathetically into the bush, hoping to lose themselves as well as us. But then, perhaps not. Perhaps they had us where they wanted us all along, moving to their own stories as we already moved to Cavenagh's.

It was while DeVilliers was gone that Tyers came on to us again, without warning and without Marlay this time but still as much of a crown official as before. Can you picture him shadowing us upstream, holding on to our heels like an anxious dog as we went about our business? He was on horseback but had held close to the river, sniffing us out until he found us. And here we were, thinking we were so far up we could not be reached.

He was playing the conscientious protector this time, moving to the stories Walsh had told him. You remember Walsh? The bold commander of the Native Police. The man with the uniforms and guns. He'd gone to Tyers, concerned that we'd upset the blacks. Upset the blacks! We'd rushed their camp, he said. Taken them against their will. Driven them into the mountains. We'd interfered with them, threatened them, taken their children hostage on the lake. You see how the story calls for absolutes. Oh yes, we were trouble — evil incarnate. And what did that make Walsh?

Good and evil; black and white. It's tempting, isn't it, to reduce it all to that — moral purpose, the clear delineation ... characters ... as if people really worked that way. They didn't want us there, you see. The story grew with every telling until Tyers, half wanting to believe perhaps, had set off in pursuit. And before long we had Walsh as well, tramping through the bush towards us with five of his police, following his own story to its natural conclusion.

You had to wonder what they thought we'd find, I mean to follow us so closely. They didn't want us snooping. Didn't want us to find her — not when they had failed.

Tyers questioned us at length. How many blacks did we have with us? Had they agreed to come? How could we be certain? Had our guns been used? Of course, he had to take us at our word — all of them were with De Villiers. (Or so we thought.) Not due back for another week. And it was DeVilliers he wanted most to talk with. We could have told him anything we wanted, spun our own fantastic stories to see how much he'd swallow. We could have kept him sitting there all night … like you are now. Yes, like you. It makes you wonder, doesn't it? These words strung together …

We didn't, though. Instead we listened to his veiled accusations and told him he was wrong. I don't know if he believed us. To this day, I couldn't say. He wrote things in his book. Issued warnings. Acted out his role, then settled to a pannikin of tea by our fire in the early evening light.

It was then that Walsh appeared, the storyteller himself. There are people you meet, you know the sort, even before they've opened their mouths to speak, you're set against them. That was Walsh. He was pleasing enough to look on: not old, not tall, not short but well proportioned with a twitchiness about him like a well-bred horse and a bristling moustache. It was like the muscles were pulled too tight inside of him. He fairly danced into our camp, holding his horse on a short rein so it skipped and champed at its bit, and he kept his knees clamped tight around its middle, never once taking his eyes off us. Just arrived, he seemed anxious to be gone. And he was always like that: his tunic tightly buttoned across his pigeon chest, his back straight. He was like a rabbit-trap, sprung and ready, and people eased their way about him in case he snapped.

Tyers persuaded him to spend the night and he set up camp a little way from us with his own men. He shared our fire, but every couple of minutes or so, he stood and looked out into the bush, or else he'd pick a piece of wood for the fire and snap it sharply against his leg. He wasn't the sort of man to waste time thinking. He was never still. His leg twitched, or he tossed twigs into the fire to watch them flare. He must have checked his horse a dozen times. And we could feel the tension he'd brought with him. The whole time he was there, it was like the rest of us had stopped our breathing.

Tyers explained to him that we'd established good relations with the blacks, but he wouldn't have it. He told us he'd long had them on his side. They trusted him. He knew all he needed about Bunjil-ee-nee. And De Villiers ... he knew all he needed to know about De Villiers too, except where he was now.

"He'll not find her by listening to them," he said. "They'll only tell him what he wants to hear." Oh, he was sure of himself alright. "Anything to keep him off their backs."

"And you're not one for tales?" I said.

"Not without foundation in the truth. They'll talk all day if you let them go and at the end you'll be no wiser."

There was some truth in what he said. How long have you been sitting here? But you see, even if I'd known then that he was right, I couldn't have brought myself to say so. It was listening he didn't like — the way it altered things, the way it took away control. Listening only complicated matters.

"Did they tell about her crying?" he asked. "And the songs?" His right knee jerked up and down as he was speaking, and when it stopped the left one started. "Oh yes, don't think we haven't heard. And did they tell about the child?" (Yes, it surprised us too.) "Did they tell about her giving birth somewhere out along the Tambo, and the other ones who'd died? And the white woman plenty, plenty cry?"

He had a piece of wood bowed tight between his hands, straining till it was fit to snap, and then he bowed it back the other way.

"And did they tell you how he tied her to a log, this Bunjil-ee-nee, to keep her from escaping? Or perhaps you didn't ask those questions. They only give you what you want."

"And who's to say it's not the truth?" I asked.

"Oh, there's truth in it," he barked, "if you can say which parts. This Bunjil-ee-nee for instance," and he snapped the stick in two and tossed both pieces on the fire. "Bunjil-ee-nee's out there. I've seen him for myself. And the longer you sat listening to them at the lakes, the further into the hills he went, and the longer I sit here listening to you the less chance there'll be of finding him at all. You're better off back in Melbourne, all of you. Coming up here, telling us how to act, passing judgment like you're God's own bloody minions." And both knees started twitching like he'd been wound up. Then he stood to stretch and paced back and forth between the horses and the fire like we'd kept him caged or hobbled him to our own misguided ventures.

"Tell your DeVilliers when you see him," he spat, "to stop his meddling." Then he looked to Tyers for support. "I'll be gone first light. For Bunjil-ee-nee. Keep them out of my way!"

"Keep them out of my way!" We were happy not to be near him at all. Happy to see him go if you want the truth. (Ah, the truth. I forgot, that's what you've come here for.)

You know he pleaded insanity for shooting William Dana? Yes, later, but it was hardly surprising when the news came out. His fellow officer! Shot him in a fit of pique when Dana tried to help him off his horse. Pushed too hard, you see. Made a fool of him in public. It was like he'd put his hand on the metal plate and ... snap ... the trap had sprung shut. Dana wore the bullet in his chest like it was a badge. Years later, it was still there, with the skin healed over and only a short, sharp pain, by all accounts, when he breathed too deep. Walsh did seven years. He could have done with seventeen.

Insanity? Who's to say? How does one decide? He went for two of our Wurundjeris with an axe. That was the second time we saw him, back at Eagle Point.

When DeVilliers returned without his namesake and discovered Walsh had been there with us, he turned and started out again to catch him up. Yes, exhausted, on foot, and with Walsh on horseback. It was foolish, but he did it. Trying to regain some face with us I'd say. He said he would catch him at Macalister's station and work with him to find Bunjil-ee-nee. Work together! Can you imagine it, how wrong he'd read things. He seemed to have lost all sense. I think he acted out of a desire to be seen at least to be doing something, fooling himself as well as us that he was still in control.

He got to Macalister's alright, only to find that Walsh had never been there. And there was nothing else for us to do but to ease the boats back into the river and let ourselves be quietly washed downstream, inevitably back to the lakes to start again.

Tyers was based at Eagle Point, a high ridge of land above the silt jetties of the Mitchell River with a good view of Lake King and the mountains. From his hut he could see the mouths of three rivers: the Tambo, the Nicholson and the Mitchell, and an arm of the lake that gave access to the ninety-mile beach. Everything was laid out below him like a map.

Walsh arrived there shortly after us, as if it was DeVilliers he'd been chasing all along.

"Returned so early?" he taunted, and DeVilliers missed his chance to ask the same of him. "Did they take you to him?"

Walsh continued. "To Bunjil-ee-nee? Did they lead you into the mountains and show you where he was?"

DeVilliers ignored him and turned towards Tyers' hut. Walsh led his horse into the police paddock where our blacks had set up camp and tethered it so close as to almost trample them. There was an acre or more he could have used, close enough to water with good feed, but he chose the spot they'd taken. He had his carbine with him. He always seemed to have it. And while he loosened his saddle straps and checked his horse's hooves, he kept it pointed at them, not aimed exactly but close enough. It might not have been charged, but then ... Even when he walked away, he swung it indiscriminately towards them.

"Those blacks are trouble," he said to DeVilliers when he came back up to the hut. "You're a fool to bring them in."

Again, DeVilliers failed to respond. It was as if all confidence had deserted him.

"They need to know who's in control," Walsh sneered.

Warman was laying out provisions in the shade, behind Walsh but near enough to hear what was being said, and he left it to take up DeVilliers' cause. "Indeed," he said. "And who is in control out here? Who do you answer to, for instance? Tyers? The Governor? Yourself?"

"The settlers have no complaints," Walsh said. "But then, it's not them you're interested in, is it, being from Melbourne and working with the papers?"

He was right on that point, about the papers I mean. It was Warman who took to sending back despatches. DeVilliers took ill and failed to put pen to paper. Failed to do much at all to tell the truth, after his humiliation in the mountains. He said it was the smell of rotting weed upset him. And there was that.

All around Eagle Point and along the silt jetties the shore was thick with it; great piles of it alive with flies and rotting in the sun. It caught in your throat, the smell I mean, and made you gag. I remember, even away from it you could taste it. You could cough it up and spit it out, but it was still there in your hair and in your clothes and in the food you ate.

DeVilliers seemed more sensitive to it than most, but I don't think that was it. I think there was something he'd lost when his namesake had walked away from him.

Warman was happy enough to take control. Most of what Cavenagh got was Warman's work, like the tree and the regular reports of where we'd been and what we'd found. It was the same for Walsh.

"We have the Governor's word that your police will co-operate with the expedition," Warman said.

"Co-operate!" Walsh sputtered. "Not interfere was how I understood it."

"If you have knowledge of Bunjil-ee-nee … "

"Oh, we all have knowledge of Bunjil-ee-nee. All you have to do is mention your woman out here and they'll tell you about Bunjil-ee-nee: he's in the mountains, he's on the Snowy, he's fathered her children, he'll swap her for twenty gins … Yes, I have plenty of information about Bunjil-ee-nee."

"We would appreciate your support," Warman said, as calm as if it was me talking to you now.

Walsh didn't like it. It was after that that he went outside again. To chop wood, he said, though there was plenty of it stacked in Tyers' yard and plenty of others to cut it if it was needed. I saw him heading back towards the horse paddock with a new axe slung across his shoulder and a cocky sort of swagger like he meant no good. I never saw that wood. I never saw him carry anything but a carbine and an axe. Later our blacks told us how he'd taken to them with it, swinging it like a club and bringing it down so close to them they thought they'd lose their toes. He was handy with it, I'm sure, for a man who rarely had the need to cut his own wood.

It was DeVilliers he really wanted. To make a fool of, you see? He never had time for Warman. It was DeVilliers he wanted to ridicule, as if it was DeVilliers alone who was responsible for the expedition. He didn't count on Warman's words, or Cavenagh's.

Yes, words. It wasn't us, you see, or even DeVilliers as a person. It was the stories he might tell — the writing down of things. If he could discredit DeVilliers — if he could undermine the stories before they reached Melbourne — and keep Tyers on side . . .

Here, read them if you want — the stories that gave us life! They're all here, all in my book: Warman's accusations, the discovery of Golgotha, the broken carbine clotted with flesh and hair; all kept for ... what? Posterity? History? I don't know. What purpose do they serve now? I've kept them all in the same way others might keep perfumed letters or gilt-edged commendations, or a cherished lock of hair. A record of an adventurous life! In Cavenagh's unmistakeable prose. Yes Cavenagh, they're as much him as Warman or anybody else. Look:

"We warn of the slaughter of the unoffending natives, by those harpies of hell, misnamed police, and I almost blush to say that one or two Europeans were not a whit behind these demi civilised wretches; but of course it will not end ..." No, it will not end. Listen, there's more if it's what you want *"... as long as such persons as Messrs Dana and Walsh are in*

command of the Native Police, nothing can stop their exter-
mination for the native blacks are the most cruel, bloodthirsty
wretches alive, and nothing gives them so much pleasure as
shooting and tomahawking the defenceless savages."

That's what Walsh was scared of. Is it what you want to
hear? Perhaps I've kept them all for you, these missives from
my misguided youth, waiting for the day I knew you would
arrive, blundering in with your seemingly innocent questions
about the past. Read them. Put them to whatever use you want.
There were others, you see, besides Walsh and Dana. Others
who knew what was going on ... who must have played a
hand in it. Your father? Yes, you see now where I'm leading.
Take them. Read them. You don't have to listen to me ram-
bling from point to half-remembered point while the story you
want to hear slips between your fingers. Yes, I know how it
works, this searching for the truth. It hardly matters what I
say. Or what you read. You'll find a way to change it, won't
you?

Don't think I haven't tangled with the past myself. I know
what I'm up against ... the sleight of hand, the slow process
of forgetting and inventing. History! Truth, you say. More the
practised art of illusion. "It's here, it's gone." Better we don't
look too close. You know what I mean, don't you? You're
doing it now, taking it all in, choosing the words you'll use to
reconstruct this little meeting; to make me look more foolish
than I know I am.

Yes, I know how it works, how it draws you in. And once
it has you, once it's shown you how things stand, there's
nothing you can do but alter it. You see, I've been there
myself; I've looked into my own past, my family's doubtful
chronicle of achievements and misdeeds. My heritage! We all

do it sooner or later — succumb to the temptation despite our better judgment. Always the curiosity. Always the possibility of something better lurking there, something altogether unexpected that will change the way we see ourselves or provide some hint of purpose beyond the slow progression of days that mark our time out here. You can't blame us. I mean, there comes a time ... There must be a moment when we see it. The future — drawing towards us, diminishing with each passing day and, with it, the chances of it ever delivering what we'd expected of it. And all the while, the past ... yes, the past grows with us. You know what I'm saying, don't you? Yes, you know. Each day it has more to offer. And we turn to it, believing it will rescue us from ourselves.

Yes, I've been there before. I know how you can count on it to surprise. Should I tell you about my family? It's not the story I wanted to hear (nor you, I suspect), but it's the one I have — my father retreating prematurely into his past, back to his childhood: senility, imbecility, dementia, call it what you like. And his father before him, the very same. Every road I followed, every avenue of investigation I pursued led to the same place, to Magdalen's. The deaths recorded in the institutional hand, the stories lingering in family lore, never to be mentioned, and all the more interesting for that.

It sounds innocent enough, doesn't it? Magdalen's, Hiram's, Foundling's. The names reveal little of their purpose. Philanthropic Institutions. Hospital. Charitable Foundation. Alms-house, even. So, you think, this is where your forefathers lived out their final days, paupers perhaps, or weak of constitution, victims of some debilitating disease. No shame in that, you tell yourself; pity perhaps, or anger at the injustice of it all. But still, nothing compared to what "Penitentiary" or

"Transported Across the Seas" would bring. The family honour is still intact, no blot that won't fade with passing years. Until you hear it mentioned, the words dripping inconsequentially from some casual observer's lips — Lunatic Asylum — and your whole past collapses before your eyes.

You see your father parading before you dressed up in emperors' clothes, shabby in imitated finery — fringed epaulettes, boots, a paper hat — the very picture of delusion. And your grandfather before that, howling at the moon perhaps, yes … you see what I mean? Not random incidents; a pattern starts to form and you begin to wonder … I'm not a young man. Do these things skip a generation? I wait for the tell-tale signs, the gradual slip of memory, the loosening of reason's grip. You believe me, don't you? These stories I'm recounting. You see what the past does; how it alters things? You see what type of man I am?

Still, I'll tell you more since we've come this far. Where were we? The papers never got it right. Yes, DeVilliers was laid up ill, breathing the putrid air into his lungs and pining for his poor lost self. Malingering some would say, while we scouted round the lakes under Tyers' watchful eyes. There was nothing we did he didn't see. Marlay kept us all on record and Walsh slunk around us waiting for us to make mistakes. Sergeant Windridge was there as well, with his Border Police in tow. As if there weren't enough uniforms and guns!

He was better than Walsh — more experienced but an official nonetheless, answerable to orders and toeing the official line. *Messrs Walsh and Dana have done everything within their power to secure the woman's freedom.* Who could say if he believed it? His job depended on it. He dragged

DeVilliers off towards the Snowy, twenty-five miles in the scorching heat with no result and DeVilliers barely strong enough to lift his feet. Co-operation, see? Marlay made a record of it in his book.

The next day, about three in the afternoon, Mr DeVilliers, Mr Cavenagh and Dr Greeves walked up from the lake with twenty other Worrigals, all smiling and rubbing their breasts to show how pleased they were to find us again. Can you imagine it? DeVilliers' christened ones! They came straight up, thinking we'd be as pleased as them. And the thing is, our own DeVilliers was. He marched out of Tyers' hut to greet them, handing over tomahawks and fish-hooks again as if his illness had all but disappeared. He didn't ask for explanations. He smiled and touched their skin and called on Hartnett to help communicate with them. What stories they had to tell!

They'd found the woman. In the mountains towards the Snowy River with Bunjil-ee-nee as they'd said. Mr DeVilliers himself had seen her. He stroked Hartnett's arm to show how close he'd been to her, how he'd touched her. Even the most sceptical amongst us felt our spirits lift. He'd touched her, not two days earlier, and here he was standing amongst us telling his story to Hartnett who translated it to us. Even McLeod listened to what he said. She seemed so close. I remember stroking my own arm, the underneath of it, and feeling the soft skin there. All seemed worthwhile. All seemed promising again. We gave them beef and silver needles, anything we had just to hear them speak of her. Yes, in words we couldn't understand. But still, they were words. And we all had our questions to ask — about her state of health, about the clothes she wore, about the colour of her hair — until each of us must have built our own picture of her out of the sounds we heard, and all the while the new Mr DeVilliers nodded and waved his hands and smiled to see us so happy and enthused. Oh yes, he told us stories; he told us what we wanted to hear alright.

He would bring her to us. He would go back out there and Bunjil-ee-nee would bring her down to the lakes. DeVilliers gave him more fish-hooks and handkerchiefs as gifts for Bunjil-ee-nee. And he wrote to her. Yes, put pen to paper. I don't know what words he used ... *White Woman? Madam? My Lady?* How should she be addressed? *Dearest? Holiest of ...?* How to find the appropriate tone? Familiarity or respect? Devotion perhaps, if it had been me who held the pen. *With fondest affection ... With love?* ... How much could one presume? He wrote for fifteen minutes in his careful hand, pondering on each word, then sealed the letter with Tyers' wax and entrusted it to his namesake. How I craved to touch that paper, to add my own devotion to the bottom of it before it was spirited away. Still, I doubt I could have steadied my hand to write. And what would she have made of it, eternal love in a hurried postscript? Yes, I can see now I was a fool. Sentimental. But then ... It was different out there, so far from home.

He took it to her straight — headed off with it clutched in his hand like a royal decree and four of his tribe following behind. Ah, to have gone with them! To have crept behind them quietly through the bush towards a glimpse of her. But no, we sat tight at the lakes, fiddled with the boats, sent a dray to Cunningham's for stores, waited. Yes, waited. We waited for three days and another night and in the end it was Walsh and Dana who went after them, not us. Walsh gathered his troops and headed off in pursuit while we sat there waiting patiently for our reply.

I'll grant, it made good press, this competition between ourselves and Walsh's party. That's how they saw it, though it was a slow involvement in any race. Look, somewhere here: *... it will now be a laudable object if ambition between the Melbourne party and the Government, to see which will wear the laurel of rescuing from a frightful captivity the hapless creature ...* Yes, it's all there, the whole task reduced to what ... a steeplechase report? Entertainment? Odds given on who'll get there first. *Anxious as we necessarily are that the little band of bold adventurers will accomplish this most desired object ...* Most desired object! Cavenagh again ... *we shall be glad to find the object accomplished by the Crown ...* Glad, yes, but without exclusive rights. They still had faith in us though ... *we are free to confess we expect the other party will be the successful one.*

And when Mr DeVilliers eventually returned, Dana and Walsh must have already been halfway up the Snowy. He'd passed the letter to her. That's what he said. Certainly, he didn't have it with him. And she'd cried, he said, when she'd read the words DeVilliers wrote, wept aloud and threw herself to the ground to think we were so close. When she'd started to write herself, holding the pencil we'd sent with her left hand he said, Bunjil-ee-nee had snatched the paper away. He'd beaten her about the head. He'd tied her leg. You see what we'd achieved with our words! All for her wanting to "yabber to whitefellow" Mr DeVilliers had said.

It was we who had done it to her. We might as well have brought the waddy down ourselves. And there was more. She was marked and scarred like a black woman, her skin laid open at some earlier time to claim her. The horror of it! We imagined her enduring her humiliation like a trial. And what did that make us? Her tormenters ... to bring such misery again? Flagellators? Scourgers? Is that what we had come for, to persecute her further?

Don't think I didn't feel remorse. Yes, I felt sorrow, anguish, shame — all that. But also, and I can admit this now (don't worry, I've done my penance all these years), a perverse pleasure at having had a hand in it. Yes, don't look so self-righteously alarmed. You can imagine it, don't pretend you can't. The sharp stones coursing through her skin, the gaping flesh, the coals and pointed sticks. Have you seen pictures of the saints — the slow and painful veneration of the flesh? And don't tell me you haven't put yourself into that picture too, that you haven't thought of the cuff and clout, the breaking on the wheel, the rack and strap, all the means of exercising power. Passion, some call it. Have you never experienced passion?

And after all that, after what we'd done to her, we pleaded with her for forgiveness. Asked for deliverance. *Pray for us sinners, now and at the hour* ... You can't imagine how much we needed her!

6

We left the next morning for the mouth of the Snowy. DeVilliers travelled overland with our blacks and a group of Worrigals. Hartnett stayed behind on Raymond Island. It was what he wanted, his chance to live with the lakes tribe — eat their food, share their fire — without the judgment and smart remarks of Warman or McLeod. And if Bunjil-ee-nee made good his promise to bring her down ... I went with Warman in the boat.

There was an entrance to the lakes, a small opening that gave access to the sea across a dreadful bar that sent the swell pitching and foaming with horrific force. Tyers advised against it. He said we'd all be lost, which might have suited him, but still ... Warman was determined. I think he'd tired of the lakes. He saw the one small opening as an avenue of escape, a last chance to prove himself before our supplies ran out or the entrance closed.

McLeod was with us when we started, and Dingle. The arm of the lake that took us to the entrance was dark and still with heavy forest and rolling hills along its shore. The water reflected the sky so clearly we saw white birds flying below us like schools of fish. We held a fine run for about two hours with the forest towering over us and not a sound to be heard. There was a series of small islands that we passed then the arm widened and the water took on a strange colour and the texture of it changed. It was more than the surface of it, more than wind brushing across it or a shift in current. When I tasted it, it was salt.

There were whirls and eddies in it where the salt water met fresh and we could feel the boat move more easily through it as if it had been lifted out of the water and skimmed precariously over it. It was an unnatural feeling, the waters mingling beneath us, the thought of freshwater fish swirling amongst those washed in from the sea. And we could hear the waves crashing over the bar a mile or more away from us. It was a sound I dreaded to hear, the water folding into itself and roaring through the entrance. It was a treacherous stretch of beach at the best of times, torn with rips, unpredictable currents threatening to wrench whatever ventured into it apart. Ninety miles of broken water and us edging our way towards it.

The wind came up from the south as we approached, tearing in from off the ocean and creasing the surface of the water so the boat bumped across it and small waves broke across our bow. We reefed the sails and tried to shelter close to shore, but there was no escaping it; the wind kept buffeting us and, ahead, we could see a great wall of water arching across the entrance. It writhed and shimmered then collapsed with an enormous thud and white foam boiled through the gap into the lake. Already another wall was building behind it.

Warman took us to the mouth of it and we could feel the power of all that water heaving beneath us. It wasn't fear I felt so much as awe, and a strange attraction to it. I could see he would take us through. McLeod was all for turning back but we'd come this far and there were moments when the gap seemed clear, as if the ocean had stopped its churning to draw breath. We pulled the boat to shore and waited.

McLeod was first out, wading in through the shallow water at the edge of the channel. It was all sand between the ocean and the lake, great dunes of it knitted together with grass and twisted scrub. The water was yellow with it. A thin film of it moved about us too, lifting each time the wind blew until the air was thick with it and our cheeks and eyes were stinging. It was all we could do to stop from breathing it into our lungs. Everything about us moved. The entrance shifted even as we watched. It was foolish to venture in, but still … I remember how the water shone.

There was a lull for a good five minutes when swells heaved through the entrance but didn't break and the wind dropped. Warman scanned the horizon for the familiar lines feathering towards us and, when all seemed relatively still, he called for the boat to be pushed back off from shore.

No sooner had we done it than the wind came up and almost tore the sail from the mast. Even in waist-deep water there was a current that gripped our keel and dragged us out through choppy water before we had time to set a course. McLeod panicked. He was out of the boat, pushing it from behind when the current took us and he flailed about, pretending to have lost his grip. He had all the time he needed to clamber aboard but he let us go. Warman called for him to hold tight but he let loose his hold and made an unconvincing show of trying to get it back, then stumbled in to shore. There was no returning for him. He was safe on dry land where I suspect he wanted to be all along, and we were feeling the pull of the sea as if it was drawing the whole lake into itself.

We moved swiftly towards the entrance. The water seemed stretched in all directions and covered with a thick foam like suds that washed about us. From the shore we'd been able to see clear through the entrance but from here even the smaller waves towered above us so all we could see was water. We seemed to be constantly in a trough. And the noise … It came at us from all directions, a hissing rumbling sound and, below us, great banks of sand shifted like living things.

Our sails were reefed tight, I remember, and Warman swung the tiller uselessly from side to side trying to control the boat. But it was out of our hands. The boat would go where the current took it. We must have been close on the bar itself when we were lifted high on an unbroken swell and saw the dark lines of water building towards us from out at sea. There would be no escaping them. Warman tried to run for the eastern side of the entrance but the boat broached and before we could swing it round again the first of the waves was pounding onto the bar.

It roared towards us. When it hit the boat Warman and Dingle were crouched below the gunnels at the stern and I … I can still see it after all these years, and feel it, the suffocating fear. I was on the opposite side towards the bow, and when the boat buckled with the force of it, I was flung headlong into the swirling water.

It took me easily to the bottom. I remember how quiet it was down there in the middle of all that movement, and how gently it tumbled me across the sand as if, once it had taken me, it could do no further harm. I kept my eyes closed and felt the water pummel me from side to side, and when I opened them I was suspended in the sand-thick water, effortlessly floating there somewhere between the surface and the bottom. There was a strange light filtering through it all. I don't know how far down I was or how far from the boat. Have you ever swum in boots? One thing, they hold you straight; there's no doubt which way you need to go. I remember I tried to kick them off and clawed towards the surface as the shadow of the second wave swept across me and I was pushed to the bottom again.

There was a moment down there, when the wave was folding over me, that I was happy to give in to it. It was the air in my lungs that hurt, not the water. And if I was to let it go, if I was to let the bright water take its place ... I thought of her, held by the same water when she'd come ashore ... how much easier it would have been for her to have drunk it in, breathed it into her like air. . . You'd think it would burn your throat, or that it would burst in with such ferocity ... But it's not like that. There was a soothing sense of release when I let it in, as if an enormous weight had been lifted from my lungs. Yes, you see, I've been that close. The fear comes afterwards, when you stop to think. I felt I was giving myself to her, and even as my eyes began to close I was drawn towards the surface again, the light growing brighter every second, and I could see the shape of her, her arms reaching down towards me with all that light radiating from her. You think I'm foolish, don't you? Too much whisky in the tea? Senility or worse? Religion! I half expected her to call my name. And as I kicked my boots away, I saw the unmistakable shape of the boat above me and Warman half out of it, leaning head and shoulders into the water to drag me up.

They pulled me, half-drowned, into the boat and forced the

water out of me. My throat burned then, like barbed wire being twisted in it, and the light was so bright I couldn't see. She seemed further away than ever. The backwash rushed us through the entrance to the open sea and all I wanted was to be back there, floating calmly up towards her waiting arms.

It took a good half day to reach the mouth of the Snowy. About three miles off it we saw DeVilliers' party on the beach. They made smoke for us and we landed. There was no sign of McLeod.

DeVilliers had heard shots the night before, some way upstream and again shortly before we'd landed. We guessed we were no more than a mile or so off Walsh and Dana's camp and we made our way towards it. Do you know the Snowy? It's broad and deep with a strong flow and we moved up it easily. We heard the shots ourselves then, ringing out clearly through the trees, and muffled shouts as well.

When the noise stopped, everything was completely still. I remember we were midstream leaning against the oars and the current held us, poised if you like, on the edge of something we hadn't faced before. They were shooting them within earshot of us! We could have gone either way. I thought DeVilliers would turn the boat around, but when no more sounds came he signalled us on, cautiously upstream. We had guns ourselves for what they were worth, but … you see … who was it we should use them on? We didn't know where we stood. I don't think DeVilliers had any idea what he would do.

When we arrived at Dana's camp they were returning from the islands further up the river. They had an old man and a woman with them, chained together at the legs with handcuffs, and three children. One of the children was tied and strapped to his mother's leg so the woman could barely move. Dana and Walsh weren't surprised to see us.

"There's no white woman here," Dana said. "We've searched. You'll not find anything."

"We heard shots," DeVilliers said.

They made no attempt to hide what they'd been up to. "We rushed their camp," Walsh said, like he was proud of his achievement. "It's the only way to get sense from them." We could smell powder and hot metal in the air even as he spoke.

They had a boy with them as well, from Bunjil-ee-nee's tribe, who'd grown up on Macalister's station. Taka-war-ren his name was. Jackie. Jackie Warren. He was terrified of Walsh, I could tell, though he went with him readily enough, guiding the police to his own people and translating if they needed. DeVilliers wanted to question the old man and woman through him, but Walsh would have nothing of it.

"You'll not learn anything we can't tell," he said. "Besides, Jackie here can't tell the truth; he don't know what it is, ay Jackie? He's full of stories about his family being shot. Always has been."

"I'd like to talk with them just the same," DeVilliers said.

"There's no white woman here. Don't you think we'd have her if there was. Jackie'll tell you. There's no white woman here."

"Still, I'd like to talk."

"Talk all you like," Walsh said. "To us."

We got our way though, afterwards. Some of our Worrigals went to the prisoners with Taka-war-ren after dark, and when they came back they were all long faces and mournful looks. They told us what we knew already — the police had been out shooting. And there were other men as well, white men who weren't police but who joined in when they knew the shooting was on. They'd been out on the islands. DeVilliers asked about the woman and Jackie shrugged his shoulders. They were his own people they'd been out shooting. He said they didn't know if there'd been a white woman there or not.

Next morning, the prisoners were gone. Taka-war-ren said they'd got away with a canoe, and Walsh and Dana laughed to hear it, seeing how two of them were still cuffed together and they had the key. DeVilliers asked them for it but they wouldn't give it up. They would have died, you see, still chained together ... or one of them would, before they got it off. Dingle went on about it being inhumane but it made no difference. Walsh was breaking camp even as we spoke, wanting to start for Eagle Point before it got too hot.

"It's their own doing," he said. "We can't be searching for them when they should have stayed."

"We'll do the searching," DeVilliers said.

But they went just the same, taking the keys with them as if to spite us. Dana was anxious to describe the river. As if we didn't know enough of rivers! Upstream, he said, it forks. And he was right about this — past the islands and the banks of wild tobacco it branched in two. He told us not to take the right-hand branch.

"It's barely navigable," he said, "after a mile or two."

He told us how it closed in on itself with thick forest overhanging the water and that we'd be better to keep to the left-hand branch where the water ran broad and deep and the banks sloped easily to it.

"Not that you'll find her there," he said. "But you can travel up it. We've been up as far as you'd want to go, and she's not there."

They'd not been gone long when we saw two canoes sliding downstream towards us. They held off for a time when they saw us but our Worrigals called them in and when they realised the police had gone they came on shore. There were four of them, all men, and two knew some words of English. They knew of us. You'd be surprised how word got round. They knew we weren't with Walsh and Dana. And they knew it was the woman had brought us there.

In the afternoon they guided us upstream past rich pasture land with not an animal grazing on it. Past the islands the banks were heavily timbered with stringy-bark and blackbutt and there was thick scrub tied with vines. Sassafras and tobacco grew wild down to the water and the air was rich with the smell of it. When the river split, we took the right-hand fork.

About a mile up there was a spot where the reeds were trampled flat. Dana was right about the forest closing in and the water shallowing, but there was more. The men in the frail canoes took us in to the trampled reeds and we drew the boats up on them. It was the sound of flies that took us to the body of a man, about thirty or maybe less, lying among the reeds. His head was split. Cut in two places. It was done with an axe by the look of it, or maybe a cavalry sword like Dana wore. He'd not been dead long, a day maybe, but there was already a smell that sent Dingle gagging into the bush.

I think he expected more of what we'd found at Golgotha but there was just the one. It was me who inspected the body. There's little to it when you've been so close. The flies lifted like a dark blanket and there were gunshot marks beneath on his chest and legs. I could see how close the gun had been — close enough to burn his flesh and push the pellets in deep.

The blacks who'd brought us kept their distance. They told us there were more shot, three of them, but there was no sign. They carry them with them, you know — their dead. Or they cut bits off them. There's no burying like us. Back at the lakes there were women with their children's hands threaded round their necks. Hartnett tried to get one but they wouldn't have it. We searched for close to an hour for the other three then pushed off again upstream. The flies were swarming before we'd gone ten feet.

Their canoes — have you seen them? They're little more than strips of bark, like curled leaves only bigger. It's not hard to pass them by. We would have kept moving if the Worrigals hadn't seen one, close in to shore, lying amongst the reeds like the river had washed it in. It was too shallow for our boats so we waded in, holding the dry reed stalks to stop from falling. The water itself was still and warm and there were frogs swallowing like they do and dragonflies skittering about us. To be honest, I prefer the open water.

It was when we all stopped and waited for things to settle that we could see it — a small disturbance in the reeds a little way upstream, like an animal was crouched there in the water, shaking. Warman had a stick with him. He moved slowly towards it, beating the reeds flat before him as he went, and the blacks closed around him in a circle with the trembling reeds its centre. We waited for the rush and panic or the wail of something frightened for its life, but all we heard was the whack, whack, whack of the stick against the reeds and then Warman was there, standing over the old man and woman who'd escaped from Walsh. They huddled together, still cuffed at the legs, waiting.

The children were gone. I don't know where. Perhaps they were lying somewhere else in the rushes or had slipped quietly into the water. I don't like to think. The woman wouldn't speak of them, thinking perhaps we'd hunt them down again and take them somewhere else. We tried all the keys we had in our possession, but none would open the cuffs. They'd been locked in good and it would take more than our frantic rattling to set them free.

The man's leg was blown up twice its size and the skin had split against the cuff. Each time we moved it he winced with pain. God knows how they walked. The woman was not much better. There were lacerations on her ankle. I swear I could see the bone show through in places. Their way was to pull hard on the cuffs and strike against the metal with stones or lumps of wood, or with their hands, to tell from the way they looked.

We took the best part of two hours to file a key DeVilliers had to fit. We put it in and pulled it out and filed it off some more And each time it slipped further in with the teeth bumping sharply over the inside of the lock. Eventually something gave and the cuffs sprang open to release them. Even then, we had to ease them off the man's leg. They were smeared with blood and Dingle flung them jangling and rattling into the bush like some primitive weapon. The last I saw they were caught high in a stringy-bark, dangling like twin nooses above the ground.

We took the two back downstream with us and they wailed when we passed the spot where the body was. Even from midstream we could hear the unmistakable hum of flies laying claim to something dead. They pointed to one of the islands where they said a camp had been disturbed and we could see the trampled grass and implements lying on the ground. No bodies though. And not a sign of life either.

Back at the mouth of the Snowy there was a group of blacks waiting for us in the shade. When they saw us, they stood and moved into the light. It was a river after all, and only a matter of time before we came back down it. They'd travelled overland from Lake King. Bunjil-ee-nee, they said, was back at the lake, on the island where Hartnett was. And the white woman was with him too!

What could we do? What would you have done? It might well have been the truth ... or just as easily ... It was a twenty-eight mile march and the sea was running high again for Warman's boat. Still, there was little choice when it came to it. Dana and Walsh would be already there. We'd no meat left and precious little else. And it was Christmas Day. I remember we prayed for her and made a damper with rough-ground wheat and bran. We swallowed it with brackish tea.

DeVilliers started before dark for Eagle Point and meant to travel late into the night. I would have gone too, but since the sea had already coughed me up once without a drowning mark, I was stuck with Warman and the boat.

We pushed it into the wide estuary the next morning and it was there, while I was making the last checks of ropes and sails and Warman was scouting the shore, that he found the carbine. It was lying half-concealed near what was once a native camp with some broken spears and the burnt remains of a flannel shirt. The gun was broken off at the stock and there was a clump of black hair, all clotted with blood, about the lock.

Do you know what force it takes to break a gun like that? It isn't lightly done.

Warman scraped his thumbnail across the metal lock and it came up clean. There was a name engraved there, the letters still caked with muck but clear enough. Slowly, he cleaned each one out, tracing the shape of it with his nail until it shone in the harsh light that reflected off the water ... But yes, you know don't you? The letters. The order they were in. You don't need me to tell you. No, you don't need me to tell you your own name.

Back at Lake King, Hartnett was still on Raymond Island. He had a basket with a plaited handle he'd woven out of reeds. He'd learnt it from the women. God knows how long it took him to do it, sitting there with them, listening to their talk. He was proud of it, you could tell. He pointed out the pattern to it, the way the soft reeds slipped beneath each other like they were made for it. And he was full of talk about the food he'd eaten — the taste and texture of shellfish from the lake (soft and sweet, he said it was, like jellied tongue), and eels with the taste of mud. His book — I remember, his book was crammed with words. He showed me: *Lohantuka, Londican, Lundegai.* "White woman," he said. "It's what they call her. All of them mean her." And he seemed so pleased with himself, as if by writing them down he'd done what we'd all set out to do.

When we first arrived back, he walked barefoot towards us along the shore. He'd left his boots back in the second boat — said he liked the feel of water against his skin. He said Bunjil-ee-nee had been there with the woman and twenty tribesmen, camped on the far side of the island. He'd seen their smoke.

"And did you speak with her?" DeVilliers asked.

"No," said Hartnett. "It wasn't wise." The lakes blacks had told him Bunjil-ee-nee would come to us when he saw fit.

"But you saw her?" DeVilliers said.

"I saw her fire. I saw the smoke from it, over there."

"And Bunjil-ee-nee."

"They told me he was there with the woman. They came down from the mountains and would have stayed if it wasn't for Walsh and Dana."

Dana and Walsh had come back from the Snowy and set out on the lake to herald their return. Hartnett had seen them firing their guns into the air, shooting indiscriminately into the bush until the whole lake resounded with their shots. Next day, the smoke was gone. The far side of the island was all silence and clear sky.

Hartnett couldn't hide his admiration for Bunjil-ee-nee. He saw it as some act of bravery, coming out of the mountains like that, staying so close on the island, as if it all but made up for him having her in the first place. He'd seen how the lakers respected him, see, how awestruck they were with the idea of him, and he couldn't help but be impressed. Me? I don't know; I still had him as some sort of monster.

You'd think, wouldn't you, that DeVilliers would have wanted to bring the whole affair into the light. What happened out there, I mean, the things we saw. You would have thought he'd want to bring them to task on it. It was his moment after all, his chance to exercise his power.

But DeVilliers was happy to keep it to himself, or to Cavenagh at least. It might have been that; letting the papers do the work. Or else he couldn't bring himself to pass judgment on what he'd found. He must have disapproved! Damn him, he must have known it was wrong. But we lingered on the island, rested our aching limbs, waited for DeVilliers to act. And in the end, it was Warman who moved to put things right, as if he'd seen how the truth might slip quietly out with the tide while we sat and watched.

Tyers was out on his rounds when we eventually went for him, off towards Green Hills somewhere. Sergeant Windridge was in charge and we went to him instead. He'd heard from Dana and Walsh, but not the full story. No, not the one we all want. That's the one you're here for now, isn't it, the full story — as if there's only one. They'd made out the Snowy was like some Sunday picnic. Butchers' picnic, I'd say, with them hard at it.

But we set him straight. Yes, we made a show of it. A formal report for the Governor's eyes. And Marlay's too. Yes, we didn't forget Marlay with his careful hand. We all but dragged him to his desk and made him write it down: *On oath, I hereby depose that on Monday afternoon, the twenty-first instant, I arrived at the Snowy River ...* And we did it all again in front of Tyers when he returned and signed it in our own uneven hands with Marlay's precious ink. It flowed so smoothly I could have wept.

7

It was all mistrust after that. We had enough food for one last trek into the mountains. Tyers agreed that Taka-war-ren would lead us in. Co-operation, see? Oh yes, he was anxious to co-operate. And Sergeant Windridge joined us, just in case. To keep an eye on things. On us, that is. You see, I have my share of scepticism. They would have rathered we were heading home.

We spent two days on the island, selecting blacks. DeVilliers took more presents and empty threats, anything to get them back on side. Word had spread back from the Snowy, you see. It seemed the wind carried it or it was passed like fire sticks from tree to tree. Whatever, it travelled quickly. Quicker than us out there.

We camped just off the beach, not far from where Hartnett stayed. I remember, the water was clear and warm with flecks of quartz or mica shining in it, and it was soft against our skin. I took to going without boots myself, just to feel it. Dingle joined me at it and we walked for what seemed hours, back and forth, and felt the soles of our feet turn soft. The air about us was warm and still and I fancied I could hear birds moving on the far side of the lake, then Hartnett was there, completely naked, striding towards the water.

He flung himself into it and swam, stroking the water with his big, white hands. Then he turned and swam back towards us. The water streamed off him when he stood.

He wasn't a well-proportioned man. His arms were long and gangly and his chest had a sunken look about it as if something had given inside of him. But then — emerging from the water like that, standing there before us in the sun — everything about him seemed somehow right. He glistened like some polished statue and shook the water from his hair with, I don't know … something … a sort of elegance I suppose you'd call it.

Yes, I know what you're thinking. Sad old man with his sodden reminiscences. Think what you like. That picture of him stays, and I haven't seen him now for close on forty years. Forty years. He's more than likely dead like all the rest. You forget, don't you, how long ago it was. For all I know, I'm the only one left.

I remember I peeled off my shirt like a thick skin and felt the sun warm across my shoulders. And Dingle did the same, folding his clothes in a neat, square pile on the beach. Then we waded out into the lake and slid smoothly beneath its surface.

It held me easily. I hung there, barely moving my arms and legs, and floated beneath the open sky. Everything was still. The Snowy seemed a long way off, as if the things we'd seen there … as if they were … I don't know, somehow less real than the warm water washing against our skin.

Oh, they happened alright. You can take my word. And you see, that's all there is to take — there was no official inquiry, no investigation. Walsh and Dana were never brought to account. It was as if the events had never happened, as if they were all washed clean away by the healing waters of the lakes.

We picked four blacks to accompany us. It wasn't easy. DeVilliers wouldn't leave till they agreed to come and Taka-war-ren told them we'd bring all the white men down from Melbourne to punish them if they didn't help. All the white men! They must have seen us sweeping down like a great white flood to swallow them. For all they knew we were part of an endless stream. Eventually, we got two lakers and two Braboowoolong from the mountains, but even then we couldn't be sure.

I remember, we checked their feet. We took them down to the water's edge and made them wash in the clear water. They bathed their feet slowly, stooping submissively to do as we asked. Then we inspected them. Hartnett rubbed his palms across their soles, feeling for cuts and callouses. The lakers' feet were soft. Hartnett said they were so soft from all that time in water they felt like children's feet. But the Braboowoolong — we couldn't be sure, you see; we had to be certain they were who they said they were. We had to feel the hard skin for ourselves.

One had cuts so deep in his soles from the sharp stones of the mountains, it was like nails had been driven into them. It satisfied Hartnett. He was on his knees, holding the black man's foot, when DeVilliers ordered him up. The gesture angered McLeod too. He refused to go to the mountains with them before they proved themselves. It seemed strange, I know, coming from the very one who'd abandoned our boat at the first sign of trouble. Oh yes, he'd come skulking back alright when it suited him. When he felt things were in control, that is.

Anyway, DeVilliers took the four blacks back to Eagle Point and gave them rations and blankets. Then he left them. Four nights I think it was, to see what they would do. He expected them to scarper, see? He thought they'd disappear as soon as they saw the chance and not come back. You couldn't have blamed them if they did. I mean, what would you have done? But they didn't, see? They were still there at the end of it, the embodiment of DeVilliers' misapprehension. Each time the sun came up they were still there, waiting for us to make a start. In the end, for all the noise he made about trust and commitment to his cause, it was McLeod who decided not to come.

We left early in the morning. We took two pack-horses weighed down with our provisions, and Taka-war-ren led us up the Omeo Road to the Tambo Crossing. Our own blacks were with us too, and the four we'd chosen and Taka-war-ren's sister. Oh yes, and Sergeant Windridge. Sergeant Windridge was there as well. DeVilliers was still officially in command, but we all knew. Things had changed, you see? Perhaps DeVilliers was right; perhaps we should have kept everything to ourselves, all the sordid, telling details that, when it came to it, people really didn't want to know at all. For all we'd seen, for all the words we'd sent back to Melbourne for Cavenagh to use, it was us who were under observation now.

We kept to the left bank of the river and climbed steadily towards the mountains. The ground crackled underfoot with fallen sticks and leaves and the air was so strong with eucalypt and the scent of peppermint gum you could fairly taste it on your tongue. There were whip-birds, I remember, sounding out like a warning of our advance and the occasional scurry of something shifting through the underbrush.

The terrain changed as we went, from sandy soil with thin grass, to clay, to stones pushed hard together like impacted teeth. Only the Tambo was a constant beside us. It gurgled and stuttered like a baby struggling to speak, then flowed smoothly away to the lakes. The sun glared off it and off the baked stones that burned through the soles of our boots. The heat was so intense I thought we'd drop. The river drew us to its banks time after time as if we couldn't get enough of its cold water into our throats and the horses all but scrambled into it

On the second day out we came to a small stream that flowed into the Tambo. The junction was unremarkable. The waters met quietly. The low banks were like rounded shoulders. There were fallen trees and open ground, some rocks worn flat and smooth and dull like the stubs of toes. We would have kept on moving without a thought, except that Taka-warren's sister stopped.

She looked around as if the place held some half-remembered significance and brushed the dirt with her feet to see what lay beneath it. When she squatted near the river bank and ran her fingers through the mess of leaves there, Hartnett squatted beside her trying to see what it was she saw. He thought there was some pattern to it, see? Or some disturbance she could interpret from the leaves. The fool, he thought she was tracking Bunjil-ee-nee.

He was still down there, holding a leaf up to the light, when she stood and told us. It was the place where the woman had given birth. To a male child, she said.

Yes, it caught me too. Not surprise so much ... no, it was

more than that. We were standing on the very spot! And Hartnett was down there fossicking through the dead leaves and trailing his fingers through the dirt.

You think we were impressed? You think we saw it as some wretched Bethlehem or something? How damned naive! You can't begin to … Even now, the very thought of it … the place, what happened there … the whole idea of it appals me.

It's not what we wanted to find, you see. Not like that. It's not how she was meant to be. Holding a child perhaps — swaddling clothes and a shining babe in arms — or else standing flat-bellied before us, all intact. But not like this. Not the physical act itself, the ruptured wailing of something brought to light. And the blood! You see how it altered things. How she could never be the same again? It was as though we'd stumbled across something we should have known all along but didn't want to see, some undeniable truth about ourselves, and everything was changed because of it.

DeVilliers pulled Hartnett up and kicked dirt back over the disturbed earth then walked away from it. If anything, it drew attention to the spot and we skirted round it while Windridge took bearings back along the river and Hartnett drew sketches in his cluttered notebook. It might have been a shallow grave we were avoiding with the broken earth strewn across it and scratchings either side of it. We left it undisturbed and moved quietly away, further into the mountains.

There were times I caught glimpses of her, have I told you, sometimes a long way off through trees or over rivers or gorges or on the far shore of one of the lakes. Other times she was closer. Once I saw her walking towards us in a white dress. I called out — to her? To DeVilliers? I don't know, to anyone — only to find she wasn't walking towards us at all but away. She was running in the opposite direction. Fleeing! And once I remember, yes, I remember I saw her half a dozen times or more in the one morning as if she was following us, always keeping the same distance between and following as we went.

You don't believe me? You think it's all imagination? That I made it up? Oh no, it wasn't us who made her. It wasn't us who brought her into being by going out there in search of her. You see, even if we hadn't acted out Cavenagh's story, if we hadn't given him something to press to the page with his hot ink, she would still have been there. Oh yes, she would have surfaced. See, look here, *The Portland Guardian* no less and *Normanby General Advertiser.* See how she sprang up unannounced in all the far-flung corners of the colony.

"There is a revival of the report that an European lady is a captive among a tribe of aborigines, in, some say, the district of Gippsland, others say, in the Portland District."

That's not Cavenagh's work, or ours. Believe me (ha!) it's nothing to do with us. It's her. She had us pegged alright. But still, we couldn't help ourselves. Duty. Obsession. Love. Call it what you like, it was our job to rescue her.

We climbed higher and higher into the mountains, still holding to the Tambo, and the bush closed hard in around us, dark and thick so the sun came down in thin lines between the trees. It was still unbearably hot. For four days we trudged on, scrambling up sharp escarpments and stopping every hundred yards or so to catch our breath. The horses' hooves struck and slipped against the sharp stones and more than once they stumbled to their knees beneath our packs. My own knees ached and burned with every step and the further we went the worse it got. I would have gladly turned and started our descent. Except … yes, you know don't you? Except for her. She still had that power to draw us on.

Eventually we could go no further. The horses needed rest. We stopped and set up camp and the lakers went off for possums while we eased the packs off the horses' suffering backs. It was close to dark when they returned. They had two of the creatures, all eyes and twisted tails, and they told us Bunjil-ee-nee's group was waiting for us upstream, not two miles from where we stood.

DeVilliers ordered us on again (before Windridge could do the same, no doubt) and we dragged ourselves further up river, leaving the horses to themselves.

It was a strange light, I remember, being so high up and the sun so low in the sky. We cast twisted shadows beside us in the water and, between the trees, there was a light so bright it seemed there was a wall of bush burning before us. We squinted into it and followed each other in a single file to keep from stumbling over.

After a mile or so we stopped and the Worrigals went ahead. Their women stayed with us. We must have been so close! I don't know what I expected. Smoke perhaps, or noise, voices murmuring through the trees, something to show how close we were. But there was nothing. Our own blacks had disappeared into the light without even the sounds of footsteps to show where they had gone.

I was ready to move again, ready to confront whatever waited for us, when DeVilliers crouched by the edge of the stream and scraped some wet clay off the rocks. He stood and looked at it, reddish brown and caked between his fingers, then slowly smeared it across his face.

And what would you have done? What would you have

made of it? I turned away. I made as if I hadn't seen him do it. But there was no escape. He stood there, half smiling, with the brown stain across his face as if he'd suddenly discovered something about himself, then he stooped again for more. By the time he'd done with it, it wasn't DeVilliers at all but someone else before us. Someone we didn't know. He might have done anything at all and we wouldn't have been surprised. Yes, I felt afraid. I'll admit to that.

He told the women to take the clay and do the same to us. He scraped it up himself, I can still remember it, and spread it on the rocks in front of them. And they did it. Yes, every man jack of us was smeared with the filthy stuff and marked with lines and circles round our eyes till any one of us would scare ourselves half to death.

Hartnett was first. He couldn't get there quick enough. He stripped off his shirt and rolled the tops of his trousers down and the women rubbed their hands across him, working the clay into his skin. How he loved it! You could see him wallowing in it; all that attention and the feel of the soft earth. He made them plaster it through his hair and across his back till he was red with it then stood there looking at DeVilliers, and DeVilliers looked back at him.

I remember how it felt. The clay held to my cheeks. The women's fingers dragged across me, heavier than I imagined with the thick ochre trailing from them. They circled my eyes and smoothed it across my brow, and the more of it they rubbed into my skin, the more I surrendered myself to them. It was as if I felt myself disappear before them, and when they'd finished they must have stared into a strangely familiar face that I could never know. The clay dried and tightened in the warm air like a new skin stretching across my bones. I might have been anyone peering out through the brown earth and drawing the scent of it in with every clogged breath I took.

When we were all done we moved on again, tentatively at first, feeling our way across the rough ground like new things, blinkered and stumbling against each other. Everything seemed at a distance from us. Voices, the calls of birds, my own footsteps, all came heavy and muffled like thick sounds through water.

The women were somewhere behind us and I could hear their voices cackling at us with each unsteady step we took as if the whole thing was some elaborate joke they'd played on us. And every time I turned to find them, there was the clay face of Hartnett or Windridge or DeVilliers instead, staring blankly back at me like a reflection of the thing I was myself.

We went like this for another half mile or so, slowly gaining confidence and feeling our way forward with our feet. We learned not to trust our eyes but felt the shape of the land instead, treading lightly over it, moving without thinking what lay ahead, always trusting that our feet would fall on firm ground until we felt there was nothing we couldn't do and nowhere we couldn't go without the scrub and rocks taking us as their own and spiriting us up the mountain.

A sign of friendship. That's what DeVilliers said it was, this concealing ourselves behind mud. Hiding our faces as a sign of trust. But the thing is, I couldn't trust what I might do myself, made up like that, acting without thinking. Anything was possible. When we joined with our own blacks again, we stopped and DeVilliers ordered us to prime and load our guns out of the women's sight (though they must have known), and we concealed them beneath a huge log within easy reach. Then we waited.

To this day, I can't remember any sound. It's as if the whole scene unfolds now, silently as it did then, before my still bewildered eyes. I might have been the first to sight them. I don't know, perhaps we all saw them at the same time, the same unforgettable moment when we realised our position. There must have been a thousand of them ... more ... streaming down from the mountain in two dark columns to a headland by the river. There seemed no end to them, as if all the tribes of Gippsland were coming down on us.

They gathered not far from where we stood, flanked shoulder to shoulder with not a word spoken and barely a footstep sounding from them. I remember there were no spears. Some of the women carried children and there was an old man with a possum cloak held about his neck, but the rest held nothing. It was strange, I couldn't say if it was us had found them, or them that had come to us. Either way, we stood still before them wondering what they'd do or whether they saw us at all behind our ochre masks.

It was Taka-war-ren spoke first. He called out in a shrill voice, "blackfellows carry him spear along him toe!"

And he was right. The long grass was prickled with them. They slid towards us, gripped between their toes, and we could see the grass quiver before them with each barbed step they took.

Windridge made for the guns but it would have been no good. They were so close, you see? So close they were all but bristling against us and we stood there, watching the ground move in front of us, waiting for them to speak.

You'd think we'd have been afraid, wouldn't you? You'd think we would have felt our skin go cold beneath the mud or else we'd sweat or shake or feel our knees go weak — any of the usual signs, the common expressions of fear. But it wasn't like that. It wasn't like that at all. I don't know what I felt, looking out at them from behind the mask as they formed themselves into an open circle. It was as if I'd removed myself from the scene and looked on from a safe distance while it was acted out in front of me.

Taka-war-ren made the first move. He recognised his own father and lunged towards him, heedless of the spears in the grass. It was a passionate meeting, you'd have to say. I don't know how long they'd been apart but they touched each other's chests and wept openly in front of us. Hartnett made some sense of what they said. The old man asked why he'd brought us to the mountains and Taka-war-ren told him we meant no harm. He told him how Macalister looked after him, and Tyers and Walsh, and when he said he'd been to Melbourne his father wept again, as if it hurt to hear his son had been so far away.

DeVilliers moved forward then with his blanked-out face and met the older men, one by one, then he scraped a line in the dirt with his foot. He told Taka-war-ren to ask the blacks to camp on one side of it and we set up our own rough camp on the other. There was no sign of Bunjil-ee-nee. No sign of the woman, though they knew well enough what it was we'd come for. Always, she was higher in the mountains. Always they would bring her when the time was right. I'm not stupid. I can see now why they did it. I can see why they didn't come straight out and deny they ever had her. It was us, you see? It was exactly what we wanted. And if they had her and were to give her up . . . What then? I can see it now, for what it's worth . . . our own stories came spinning back on us the way we'd always told them, as if they knew all along it was our own voices we wanted so much to hear.

That night, DeVilliers told our blacks to give a ceremonial dance, and when it was under way he pranced into the firelight himself, jerking his trousered legs in foolish imitation, and Hartnett joined him too with his dangling arms and heavy-footed steps. Even with the mask I couldn't do it. The mountain blacks laughed and rocked from side to side in wide-eyed disbelief. They must have wondered what they'd struck, after Dana's guns and the whisperings from the Snowy. Here at last was the White Woman Expedition, all the way from Melbourne, putting on a show.

They obliged by dancing for us too, and when they were done DeVilliers asked about the woman. Oh yes, they knew where the woman was; had great respect for her. Bunjil-ee-nee kept her higher in the mountains. At first light they would bring her to us. All we had to do was wait.

I don't know how much of it DeVilliers believed. Windridge took them at their word. I might have too, at the time. You have to remember how close we were; how far we'd come; how desperately we wanted her. And the hunger! Our rations were all but gone. Do you know what hunger does — how it clouds your judgment? But then again, perhaps DeVilliers knew all along what we could hope to find. Perhaps, behind his foolish mask, he'd already found it.

Next morning they sent two Braboowoolong to fetch her. No sooner had they gone than a sort of restless panic moved through the blacks' camp like wind moving across the water. They watched each other. They watched us. The young men stood as if ready to leave then squatted again with their spears at hand. And each time one of us ventured to the river bank we heard a murmuring between them. When DeVilliers went to slake his thirst, two men followed close behind like altar boys shadowing a priest. They scooped up sand and sprinkled it in his footsteps then smoothed it over so there was no sign. It was as if he'd floated above the ground.

Fear, Hartnett said. Not of us but of what would happen if DeVilliers was harmed.

When the two returned some of the younger men shifted uneasily towards the trees, anxious to be gone it seemed, fearful that something was about to happen.

The woman wasn't with them. I need hardly say it, do I? They pointed to a line of trees on a ridge some miles away, all watery and twisted with the heat. She was there with Bunjil-ee-nee and he wouldn't give her up. Who knows if it was true? The ground was all but impassable — rough with broken stones and fallen trees and scrub so thick it would have been impossible to force our way through. They might have gone there. They might have found a way in and spoken to her, but then ... they were back so quick you see. It would have taken us all day.

They offered one of their own gins if we'd leave — if we'd let Bunjil-ee-nee keep her. And all the while the young men kept slinking off into the bush until there was barely a handful left. The woman they offered stood quietly beside her mother. She was small and slight — barely more than a child with undeveloped breasts — and she stared at us sullenly, daring us to take her. You see how foolish the whole thing had become? You see what we'd entered into, unwittingly perhaps — the happy band of bold adventurers!

Windridge was all for going on. He shouted at the blacks to take us to her or we'd use the guns and they told us we were too much sulky with them. That's what they said. They thought we'd shoot them anyway, you see, as soon as we had the woman. Who knows? They might have had it right. I can't speak for Windridge.

It was DeVilliers who gave the order to turn back. Yes, DeVilliers.

"It's not my wish," he said, "that you should go without water."

It was true, there'd have been no water if we persevered, and precious little feed for the horses, not to mention us. We'd have had to leave the river. And who knows how long it would have taken us? "It's not my wish," he kept repeating, and he turned with a sort of sad decisiveness to start the slow descent to the lakes again. It was over for him, that much was clear. It might have been the sight of the young girl standing there before him, but if truth be told, I think he knew how it would end all along.

Windridge wouldn't have it. He tried to spur us on, filling the air with words of encouragement. "Where blacks can go …" he said, but the thing is we had no idea where they'd gone at all. There was only a handful of them left. And the girl. She stood dumbly beside her mother, waiting to see what choice we'd make.

In the end, I sided with DeVilliers. There was little we could do … so far up with only the river to guide us in and still no clear sign that she was there. I turned my back on the girl and followed him downstream.

Back to Eagle Point we went, back to Tyers, back to Marlay's self-righteous little smirk. Oh yes, he had his day, I'll give him that. We might have stayed. We might have headed out again. I don't know, DeVilliers seemed too readily defeated. And when Tyers refused us credit on our rations there was nothing for it but to keep on going — back to Melbourne, back to Cavenagh empty-handed, limping into town like an inconclusive story. The inglorious return of the bold adventurers!

Cavenagh made of it what he could, built it into something vaguely better than it was. Oh yes, he kept the fires burning. See here:

"The attempt to liberate the unfortunate captive from her savage thraldom and brutal subserviency, was abandoned only when all hopes of success by stratagem had ceased … Our small but intrepid band therefore was compelled to retreat when they felt the inadequacy of their force to maintain a position of defence which any harsh measure must have rendered inevitable. All of them, however, are still anxious to renew the expedition, and even if unsupported by the public, have resolved on their own responsibility to recommence their labours, feeling most thoroughly satisfied that perseverance, prudence, and resolution eventually will crown their efforts with success."

"Crown their efforts with success!" I can laugh now. I can see the folly of it all. But then . . .Yes, she was still out there then. And where were we? Back in Melbourne where we'd started.

8

Don't despair, I've not forgot your father. I'm not done yet by a long shot. There was something we brought back.

Yes, he was out there with Walsh and Dana. He was on the Snowy when they were putting things to rights. And at Golgotha more than likely. Not that he said as much. Not that he needed to. And he'd been out before that too, you see, volunteering his services whenever there was a little sortie underway. You have to remember, he was a useful sort of man — strong, handy with a carbine, quiet. Yes, I'll give him that. You could count on him to keep his mouth shut. But you'd know that, wouldn't you? How little he had to say. That's why you're here, all ears and disbelief, finding it out from me.

I kept the faith, you see. DeVilliers would have nothing to do with the second expedition, but I went out there again. Couldn't help myself. Perseverance, resolution? I don't know, foolishness perhaps. I wanted to sleep at nights. Each time I closed my eyes I saw her, calling out from behind the line of trees, or pricked with spears in the natives' camp, waiting for us to come. And there was nothing for it but to go.

I met your father on the boat. We slung our hammocks

together above the boxes of trinkets we'd taken for the blacks: fish-hooks, jews' harps, sailors' knives, a dozen tomahawks wrapped in cloth. Mirrors. All night we swung above them, listening to their tinkling chatter as the ship pitched and yawled in the heavy swell, and by morning some unspoken bond had been forged between us.

We didn't mention her. We both knew why we'd come. She justified everything, you see. More than likely we dreamed the same erratic dreams of her, both held her close to us as we slept. That much we understood.

But you're not convinced, are you? You're not convinced faith could be that strong. I know, you want hard, cold evidence? Some artefact to lift her out of my faltering memory and place her … where? Firmly in the tangible world of fact?

Yes, I know how the argument goes; you want a place for her in history. And not just history but in your own petty story — the unremarkable history of your anonymous forebears. Yes, I know. It comes with living in a new country, this trying to forge a satisfactory past — valour, glory, noble deeds. Better not to scratch too deep I think.

It's evidence you want. Yes, something to hold her by. Something for the unbelievers. It's hardly fashionable now, is it, this belief? This unquestioning faith of ours. It belongs to the past too. But you see, the evidence changes nothing. If I tossed these pages — all these yellowed clippings carefully pasted from the papers, all the tentative reports of her — if I tossed them into the fire now and watched them burn, nothing about the past would change. The stories would still be told. She'd still be there.

I'll give you evidence. Here, I still have it, folded away somewhere, yes safely away, look at it. Yes, you see it. Don't seem so unimpressed. I'll grant you, in this dim light it's hardly a holy shroud — little more than a tattered piece of rag, a handkerchief perhaps, salvaged from God knows where and pressed like a flower between these pages.

But look close, feel the texture of it between your fingers, the elaborate stitching, see the faded letters printed on it. Do you recognise the words? Can you make them out? No, I thought not. You've no language. Too sceptical you are, too anxious for the cold hard facts.

Tha fichead fear, wuld dlubh geal agus cuid ...

It might just as well sound off stone. But you see, for all we knew, it might have been her language. There were plenty were convinced it was. Imagine it, when she came across them, her own tongue flapping in the breeze from the limb of some wretched tree in the incomprehensible bush. How it would have sung to her!

Pure white, the linen was, when we strung it through the bush. Yes, that's right, and not just one but scores of them. Spread like flags they were, in the hope she'd stumble onto them. Don't worry, I won't keep you in suspense. See here, where the print has faded. Yes, the mother tongue you'd call it. We considered all possibilities. Here, hold it against the light, I'll read it. There was a time I knew it word for word.

"White Woman: There are fourteen armed men, partly White and partly Black, in search of you. Be cautious; and rush to them when you see them near you. Be particularly on the look out every dawn of morning for it is then that the party are in the hopes of rescuing you. The white settlement is towards the setting sun."

"The white settlement is towards the setting sun." The irony of it. They must still be there, our rags, or what remains of

them: the wretched shreds still hanging from the trees. Such folly. Such desperation. And it wasn't only rags. There were mirrors too. The same ones we slept above. Yes, we decked the forest with them, your father and me, flashing shards of glass that shone through the scrub to confound the blacks. I remember, we stumbled across them ourselves on our way back in, scores of glinting eyes that threw our reflections back at us as we passed.

Picture it — all that shining glass. All that light. And what would she have thought when she came across them? When she peered in to see her own tormented face staring back at her? To think we could have been so cruel, so vindictive. Better she should never have seen a glass again! And worse, each one had that same message etched into its back, *Tha fichead fear*, to remind her what she'd been.

It didn't take us long to bring the great Bunjil-ee-nee in. Yes, we found him easy enough, after all our efforts with DeVilliers. He was on Lake King, waiting, and the lakers took us to him straight as if it was nothing more than an appointment with a petty clerk. The great chief, we had him pegged as. King of all Gippsland.

When we arrived, he was sitting by a small fire with two women and half a dozen tribesmen. He was impressive enough to look on, I'll give him that. A straight back and solid head. About forty-five he was, with scars across his chest and a way of holding the other blacks in place. And the thing is, he seemed unconcerned to see us. It was as if he was happy we were there. He took our fish-hooks. He ate our meat. He peered into the mirrors with a smug satisfaction at what he saw. Everything seemed to please him, everything we damned well said or did.

We even played the bag-pipes for him. There was a fellow had them with him. Imagine it, squeezing the wind out of them by the lake. And for three nights we listened to him play while Bunjil-ee-nee smiled and nodded, smiled and nodded and we waited for the right time to ask about the woman. It was the fish-hooks though that caught me, the way he closed his fist on them, the way he took them without any thought of how small they made him look.

In the end Sergeant Windridge asked him where she was. He spoke alright. Taka-war-ren put the questions to him and he answered every one. It was his story then, you see. He knew he had us. All we could do was listen. She came ashore one summer, he said, with ten men. All of them were dead. She'd had five children — all boys except the first, which they'd killed. I don't know what he wanted. Anger. Disbelief. He kept on talking as if it was the story we were there for. Anything to hold our interest.

She was in the mountains with his brother. She was on the Tambo near Numblamungie. He would send to bring her down. All lies. All fabrication. How many times had we heard it? And then he told us — and this is where things changed — he told us of another woman. Another woman from the same boat. And we could have her!

So tell me, what would you have done? How long would you have sat there waiting? He described her for us, told us how they'd dragged her in through the breaking waves — a white woman with curly hair beneath a cap. And bright eyes. See them carrying her across the foam, holding her aloft. There were deep wounds along her sides, he told us. And her arms cut off beneath the elbows. Yes, you see don't you? You see what it was they'd found.

"*Him carry one big waddy like him Corong stick,*" he said.

And he held three fingers up to show the shape of it. Yes, you can imagine the joy we felt. Britannia herself, there in the shifting dunes behind Lake King! He could take us to her. They had her hidden in the sand. Danced around her for all we knew.

Just the thought of her was enough to lift our spirits. To know that she'd survived — she of all things — and was there, so far out, keeping watch over the quiet land. And he'd take us to her! Who'd have contemplated it, who'd have thought how quickly things could change? I felt like bending my knees in gratitude to him for delivering us to her.

There was a ceremony that night, dancing and more playing of the pipes, and Bunjil-ee-nee exchanged his name with one of our party. All the blacks, he said, would honour him now he had his name, and all his kin would be to Bunjil-ee-nee what they'd been to him. We shrugged off our fears. All our apprehensions seemed to disappear with the wailing of the pipes that drifted out across the lakes.

In the morning Tyers came and took him in. The fool! Bunjil-ee-nee went willingly enough. Saw it as an extension of our kindness no doubt, a reward perhaps for what he'd told us. Whatever, he was marched unceremoniously away to the paddocks at Eagle Point and held in custody with his wives. His Majesty, the far-famed Bunjil-ee-nee, held with the horses behind Tyers' unsatisfactory fence.

He signed a treaty with them. *Memorandum of agreement,* they called it. *Entered into this day between Charles J. Tyers Esqr. J.P. on the part of Her Majesty's Government, and Bunjil-ee-nee, Chief of the Gipps Land Tribes.* I should know;

I put my name to it. I witnessed it beneath his own rough mark and watched them press the seal. *I, Bunjil-ee-nee* ... would he have recognised his own name even? ... *promise to deliver the white female residing with the Gipps Land Blacks, provided a party of Whites and Western Port Blacks proceed with me to the mountains at as Early a day as may be convenient for the purpose of obtaining her from my Brother.* And that wasn't all. No, it didn't finish there. *I also agree to leave my two wives and two children with the said Charles J. Tyers as hostages for the fulfilment of my promise.*

And what did we offer in return, *on the part of Her Majesty's Government*? Think of it. What was she worth to us after all we'd gone through? What price did we put on her that day when all but our faintest hopes of finding her had dwindled? ... *one boat with oars, a Tent, four Blankets, a Guernsey frock, some fish- hooks and a fishing line ... and a Tomahawk for the said Bunjil-ee-nee's own use.*

That's what it had come to. And DeVilliers' debts still unpaid at the Government store.

We searched for the figurehead. By God we searched for it. Each time they told us where it was we traipsed into the dunes, convinced we'd find it. And each time we came back empty-handed.

Everything was deception. The land rose and fell like the sea itself, constantly moving, scooped into hollows by the wind and held with spinifex and spider-grass that scratched us through the fabric of our trousers. Each hollow looked the same, each clump of grass, each stunted bush we passed. So each day, when we resumed our search ... You see, we couldn't tell. She might have lain there half concealed beneath our feet, or behind a clump of bush we turned our backs on for its likeness to one we'd seen the day before. We lurched and stumbled from spot to spot.

In the afternoons the sun was so fierce it burnt us through our clothes. The whole place shimmered with heat. The sand glared like a million particles of glass into our uncomprehending eyes until they streamed with tears. And all along there was the thought that the blacks had moved her in the night, that the whole thing was some game to them and she was lying in the open, staring blank-eyed into the sun in the precise spot we'd looked the day before. There were no signs, you see. Nothing for us to follow, no footsteps in the drifting sand, no trail of something heavy dragged from place to place while we slept.

I can see now what it had become — more than a distraction, more than a poor replica of what we'd set out to find. It was the very thing itself — a flawless piece of work, the wood smooth and shining, blazing white with polished paint and gold robes flowing from her shoulders. Proud eyes. The perfect face. I can see now how wrong we were.

And it wasn't that we thought, in finding it, we might somehow move closer to finding *her*. It wasn't even that it might answer unspoken questions about her, or alleviate us of the duty of bringing something back at least. No, the truth is, we quite forgot the object of our search.

Even as we stumbled through the dunes she might have been calling out for us in the mountains, trusting that we'd come. It hurts me now to think of it.

Oh yes, we found it in the end. But then, you'd know that. It was only a matter of time, you see, before we came across it, broken, lying face down in the sand. And what a tawdry prize it was — not white at all but painted green and copper, both breasts cut with some blunt instrument, nail marks, a hole in each temple where it had been fastened and wrenched away. A shabby decoy really, no use to us at all but to feed the fire.

Still, we danced with joy to find it. Yes, danced. What exhileration as we lifted it shoulder high and felt its rough wood against our backs. Yes, we brought it in — would have carried it to Melbourne if we could. How self-satisfied we felt, how proud. How it made up for all we'd been through — to be bearing Britannia back to civilisation.

And the thing is, not for a second did I see it for what it was: the horrific replica of her, the shadow image of the woman herself who, for all we knew, bore the same scars, the same mutilations, had the same stark eyes staring out of a head that no longer felt the shame inflicted on it. Not for a minute did I see the image that I see now, of the White Woman herself being carried, shoulder high, by a band of men not unlike ourselves, in the opposite direction.

That night we drank sugar with our tea. Tyers erected her outside his hut, propped her up with sticks to stare out across the lake, and all night she was there with us, glowing with the reflection of the fire, her trident raised, watching over us with her unclosing eyes as we slept.

Your father couldn't keep his hands off her. If it's truth you want, she satisfied all his needs. From the moment we brought her in, his job was done. Each morning we'd find him with it, smoothing back the wood, caressing it, plugging the holes with gum. Tyers issued paint from the government store and he daubed it on her, made her shine again like she was his own creation. He might have slept with her for all we knew! And when time came for Bunjil-ee-nee to lead us to the mountains, there was nothing we could do to draw him away from her.

Yes, we made one last trip for her. Winter was closing in by the time we left and there was snow on the higher peaks. Three months we'd been out there and nothing but the figurehead to show. We made our way out slowly. Bunjil-ee-nee shuffled in front of us, long-faced, surly, not wanting to be in the mountains at that time of year. His legs hurt, he said. There were pains in his feet that made him go so slow.

It was clear from the start we wouldn't find her. Still, we persevered. It was bitter cold, and the higher up we got the harder it became to see for cloud and mist. One night it snowed and we woke to find ourselves dusted with it and the whole land white and shining about us. The ground was hard and slippery beneath our feet. Bunjil-ee-nee led us on a winding course, hobbling over rocks and stones for sympathy. We crossed from ridge to ridge, doubled back on our own tracks, kept returning to the river, and all the while he kept his eyes averted from us.

In the end we came to a place where a large log lay beside the river. Part of it was burnt and there were straps of plaited grass still fastened to it where something had been tied. Bunjil-ee-nee refused to speak. Even our own blacks noticed how his temper changed, how he sulked and turned away from it as if anxious to be gone. And when Taka-war-ren told us it was where he'd held the woman, he walked away from us — smug, happy with himself — as if, by taking us there, he'd given us what we wanted.

Yes, he thought we'd be satisfied with that. The log, the ropes — proof that she'd once been there. But you see, it wasn't proof we wanted. We weren't like you. It wasn't that we ever doubted her existence. I remember I touched the ropes. They were soft and pliable, came easily away in my hand, but then who could say how long they'd lain there? The ends of them were frayed like hair.

There was nothing else. We could have followed him round in circles till we perished in the cold. We could have pushed on for what — another mile, another two before the cloud closed in so thick we couldn't see? No, he'd shown us all he had to show. It was the end of it, you see? There was nothing else for us to do.

We told him we'd take him back to Melbourne to be hanged. All the blacks, we said, would be hunted down and shot. It made no difference. He wouldn't give her up. All he wanted was his wives and sons to travel with him.

So yes, we took him in. How they must have laughed. How they must have smirked behind their hands to see us coming, half-starved, caked with dirt, stumbling back into town with a black man in tow. Not a glorious prize at all but the very wretch who'd duped us. Bunjil-ee-no Boy. The great man! Lady killer! How Cavenagh had built him up. And here he was, not even in chains, not even an impressive public spectacle, with his two wives following quietly behind. You see what we'd brought them? The monster himself reduced to a wretched black man shuffling his feet through the dust. The very opposite of what we'd set out to find.

No, we didn't hang him. We denied them even that. There was no need, you see, for such theatrics (the mask, the twitching dance). There are many ways to kill a man. We held him in custody instead. Under guard at first — a sentry on the watch-house door, two hours exercise a day. Then in Tailor's shop with rations for his wives and children. And all the while he grew more melancholy for being held.

He never spoke of her again, never told us where we'd find her. And in the end, he died at Narre Warren in the paddocks where they held him. Twenty months it was, since we brought him in. And her still out there.

So, are all your questions answered? Are you any better off for what you've heard? No, I thought not. Nothing's changed. It's not the history you wanted, is it? Not the past you'd choose. Still, it's easily forgotten. I'm an old man; dementia in the family. You could write your own for all I care and, when it comes to it, no one need ever know. Yes, we'll keep it to ourselves, will we? It's for the best. And when I'm gone … Yes, when I'm gone … Well, you've got your story … and when we're said and done, that's all there really is.

Also by Liam Davison

Soundings

Winner: NBC Banjo Award for Fiction 1993

This bold and impressive novel interweaves narrative strands from past and present to create a world that is familiar yet disturbingly strange. Landscape becomes an obsession, photographs throw up unsettling images distilled from the past, reality and imagination begin to shift ...

"The writing is tense, inexorable and very moving. This is an Australian novel you don't pass by."

Gerard Windsor, *Weekend Australian*

"A truly striking and beautifully crafted work ... a highly recommended and enjoyable read."

Rod Moran, *West Australian*

"*Soundings* is writing about writing about history and it works marvellously ... This is, to my way of seeing, an important book."

Nigel Krauth, *Australian Book Review*

"Davison imaginatively invites us to discover our present by reinventing our past ... he challenges us to imagine and understand the ways in which seeing is also inventing and possessing."

John Hanrahan, *Age*

ISBN 0 7022 2462 6

The Shipwreck Party

At a party on the sinking *Hydra*, a guest discovers a strange secret floating at the heart of the ship. In other stories, the trail of an elusive father is lost in a series of photographs, and a child standing in Greenwich observatory overhears the filtered conversations of an illicit love affair. Through portholes, diving bells and telescopes, the characters in these fourteen short stories watch a world that is rich with suggestion and hidden meanings.

In luminous, subtle glimpses of the Australian coastline and in sparse, evocative glimpses of the continent's hinterlands, themes of travel and transcendence, discovery and disappearance shift from the sea to the land and its people. Liam Davison's first collection reveals a new creative voice which journeys through time and inheritance to explore the significance of human experience in an evanescent landscape.

"He writes in the confident tone of the custodian of the narrative. Every word feels inevitable and necessary."

David English, *Australian*

"… highly evocative writing which moves easily among elusive and peripheral moments."

Helen Daniel, *Overland*

"Liam Davison is a bit of a magician, fashioning haunting worlds of water and sand that change our sense of Australian landscape and history."

Janette Turner Hospital

ISBN 0 7022 2192 9